'No, I don't want that—let me go, Adam—*please*!'

Adam was completely taken aback at the violence of Jan's rejection. One moment she had been soft and yielding, now she was fighting him like an angry cat.

'What's the matter with you?' he demanded furiously.

'I told you I didn't like being pawed at parties.'

'You didn't mind at first—I swear it. And you said you didn't like necking with casual pick-ups. I'm not a stranger—I'm someone you see every day.'

Jan took a step backwards and faced him, whipping up her anger as she did so. 'There's another category of men I don't like being messed about by—*married* men! And you can't deny you're one of those.'

Clare Lavenham was born and brought up in London, but she has spent most of her life in Suffolk. She is married and has a son and a daughter who was a nurse at the London Hospital. She has written articles, short stories and one-act plays, but it was because of her work as a hospital librarian that she turned to writing Doctor Nurse Romances. She gets her backgrounds from her library work and consults various medical friends when necessary. Her favourite occupations, apart from writing, are walking in the country and gardening.

Young Doctor Latham is Clare Lavenham's thirteenth Doctor Nurse Romance.

YOUNG DOCTOR LATHAM

BY

CLARE LAVENHAM

MILLS & BOON LIMITED
ETON HOUSE   18-24 PARADISE ROAD
RICHMOND   SURREY   TW9 1SR

First published in Great Britain 1989
by Mills & Boon Limited

© Clare Lavenham 1989

Australian copyright 1989
Philippine copyright 1989
This edition 1989

ISBN 0 263 76421 4

Set in Plantin 12 on 12 pt.
03–8905–48683

Typeset in Great Britain by JCL Graphics, Bristol

Made and printed in Great Britain

CHAPTER ONE

SLOWLY and carefully the surgeon's skilled fingers peeled back the chest to reveal the heart. It lay there before them, warm, red and alive, its powerful muscle still pumping arterial blood into the owner's circulation system.

It was the first time Jan had assisted at a cardiac operation and she found it thrilling, even though her boss had assured her this was no more than a routine repair job, a mere matter of putting right a faulty valve.

That was two weeks ago. Now the patient was sitting up in bed, pink and healthy-looking and asking when he could go home.

'Perhaps you'll be good enough to give us the benefit of your opinion, Dr Latham?'

The quiet voice of the heart specialist was superficially courteous, but the underlying sarcasm was unmistakable. It sliced through Jan's momentary absorption in her own weariness and she winced as she felt the impact of his displeasure. What on earth had Mr Delaney asked her? She hadn't a clue!

What a fool she'd been to let her mind wander during the round on a day when Adam Delaney obviously needed careful handling. He wasn't often in a bad mood—usually both patients and

staff found him charming—but every now and
then he was like dynamite, ready to explode at the
slightest provocation.

And yet it wasn't entirely her fault she'd been
absentminded. She was so tired she could hardly
keep her eyes open. Last night had been a prime
example of what a young hospital doctor was
supposed to be able to take in his—or her—stride,
called out three times, her sleep scarcely totalling
four hours.

Across the patient's bed she caught a
sympathetic glance from Peter Felgate, the
charge nurse responsible for Simpson and
Nightingale wards. She and Peter had been
friends from the age of five, and next-door
neighbours for a time as well. Peter had wanted
to be a doctor too, but a widowed and much-loved
mother had caused him to settle for nursing
instead. They had met seldom during the long
years of Jan's medical training, but now she had
returned to her home town they had met up again
at Amberwell Hospital.

Jan pulled herself together and faced Adam
Delaney's steely dark blue gaze with as much
courage as she could muster, although she was
uncomfortably aware of flushed cheeks.

'I'm sorry, Mr Delaney. Would you mind
repeating the question?'

'I was asking—' he spoke slowly and carefully,
as though to a particularly half-witted student
'—whether in your opinion Mr Norbury is now
ready to be moved to the Rehabilitation

Unit?'

Fortunately it was a question which Jan had already considered in conversation with the patient. He was elderly and he lived alone—he wouldn't find life easy after the heart attack which had landed him in hospital. But, on the other hand, he had determination and an independent outlook, and would do his utmost to adjust to living life at a slower pace.

'Yes, I do think so, sir.' She smiled at the old man and was rewarded by an answering gleam from the faded eyes. 'I know Mr Norbury is longing to get back to his own home and——'

'I'm aware of that, Dr Latham,' Adam Delaney interrupted impatiently. 'It was a medical opinion I was asking for, not a sentimental evaluation of a situation which is nothing in the least out of the ordinary. Almost without exception patients long to return home, in spite of all the efforts we make to ensure their comfort in hospital.'

Standing at the foot of the bed, Tim Robertson, the registrar, a cheerful young man with a ginger beard, now intervened. 'It's only natural, sir, don't you think?'

Adam Delaney shrugged and made no reply. His brilliant eyes under the long dark lashes were fixed on Jan's face. He was obviously still waiting for the medical opinion.

Jan hesitated and then took the plunge. 'Mr Norbury's pulse and respiration chart shows wonderful improvement. I really think he's ready for rehabilitation.'

'I agree with you, doctor. I should like you to make arrangements today, please.'

'Yes, sir.' She drew a long breath of relief because the ordeal was apparently over. Following the others to the next bed, she made up her mind to concentrate like mad for what remained of the round and thus—she hoped—avoid trouble.

They finished in Lister and went on to Nightingale, the women's ward. Although Peter was responsible for it, he did little actual nursing here, relying on his staff nurses to provide patient care.

'Caroline Garnham's back again, sir,' the charge nurse said as they entered. 'Admitted yesterday evening.'

'I had already heard, thank you,' Adam told him curtly.

But as he advanced towards the first bed, where a pretty seventeen-year-old girl was propped up by pillows, his whole manner changed. 'Hi, Caroline! So you couldn't stay away from us, then?' he asked, smiling.

'Afraid not, Mr Delaney.' She grimaced down at the terminals of the heart monitor which decorated her chest. 'It's less than two months this time.'

'Never mind, we'll get this tiresome heart of yours under control eventually. You'll just have to be patient, love, and that's not easy at your age.' He picked up her chart and studied it, then put his fingers on the thin wrist.

With her corn-coloured hair, large blue eyes and transparent skin, the girl would have been really beautiful if her lips had not had such a telltale bluish tinge. Her obvious fragility made Jan feel like a young carthorse beside a delicate fawn, and her own robust health embarrassed her.

Later on, when the ward round was finished and they had gathered in Peter's office for coffee, she was glad to note that her boss's black mood seemed to be wearing off. Nevertheless, she did her best to keep a low profile and merely sipped her much-needed coffee while the others discussed the various cases.

Suddenly the spotlight was on her again.

'I hope you've been listening, Dr Latham?' Adam scanned her face suspiciously.

'Oh yes, sir——'

'Because I shall expect you to be particularly watchful where Caroline's concerned. I don't for a moment suppose you've realised how seriously ill she is. Her heart is in a deplorable condition and, to be frank, the poor child's only hope is a transplant.'

Before Jan's mental vision there flashed a picture of the lovely fragile girl. Surely she couldn't be going to die? She was so pretty and so young—they mustn't let it happen!

'You'll be able to fix up a transplant for her, won't you, sir?' she asked eagerly.

He sighed and his lean dark face was sombre as

he answered the question. 'New hearts can't be purchased at the supermarket, doctor. It's not nearly as easy as you seem to imagine. We shall have to hope for the best.'

The conference ended then and Jan, greatly restored by coffee, went off to the Rehabilitation Unit. There was no problem about getting Mr Norbury moved there and she sped back to Lister to give him the good news. As she entered the area between the two wards where the nurses' station was situated, Peter came out of his office to waylay her.

'OK?' he asked.

'Yes, they can fit him in and he'll be tremendously pleased, I expect. I don't think he'll take long to learn how to conserve his energy and——'

'I wasn't thinking of Mr Norbury. I asked whether *you* were OK.' Beneath the thick thatch of light brown hair, his grey-blue eyes studied her closely. 'I don't know when I've seen you looking so tired, Jan.'

'It's hardly surprising—I've had three broken nights this week.' Suddenly irritated by his concern, she added impatiently, 'Don't you know you should never tell a girl she's looking tired? It's only a different way of saying she looks plain.'

'I'd never say that about you.'

His eyes wandered to the bright chestnut hair which she wore demurely tied back with a black ribbon when she was working, and to the round, slightly freckled face beneath it with its short nose and determined chin. Her eyes, heavily shadowed now, were hazel with vivid flecks of green and her mouth needed no lipstick to emphasise its passionate redness.

'Have you any time off today?' Peter asked quickly, seeing her on the verge of flight.

'Two hours this evening. Tim has promised to cover for me so I can go home and see my father.'

'It would be more sensible if you got a nap.'

The reddish gleam in Jan's hair suddenly justified its existence as her temper flashed. 'For goodness' sake, Peter, will you stop mothering me! I haven't seen Dad for nearly a week and you know perfectly well I like to keep an eye on him. He manages wonderfully well, but things *could* go wrong, specially now he's so busy getting his boat ready to go in the water.'

'It's amazing that he can still keep up his sailing.'

'Of course it is, but I hope you'll never tell him so. He likes people to take it for granted he can do things, not marvel at it. That way he can pretend to himself he's no different from anyone else.'

Peter looked dubious, but he made no comment, since Jan seemed in a mood to fly off the handle at the slightest provocation. It was because she was so tired, he told himself, not because she felt he no longer had a right to an interest in her welfare. He had treasured that right ever since he had defended her against the tormenting of an older boy at primary school.

Apart from his nursing, it was the most important thing in his life, but he had no illusions about Jan's attitude. He could only hope that in the not too distant future her undoubted affection would deepen into something stronger.

'I mustn't stand here talking to you,' she went on. 'I'll just have a word with Mr Norbury and then be on my way.'

After that the day began to gather speed, and once or twice she wondered if she would be able to snatch the coveted two hours off.

'Of course you'll manage it,' Tim assured her, 'I shall make it my personal duty to ensure that you do. If the Health Service wasn't so mean we wouldn't be so short-staffed. Delaney should have two registrars and two house surgeons, not just you and me.'

'If Amberwell was a larger hospital, I suppose he would have them, but actually I quite like it being this size. It's big enough to be interesting but not so huge you feel nobody'd notice if you got lost and wandered for days. The London hospital where I did my first houseman job was like that. I never did learn it all.'

'No problems like that here.' Tim looked at his watch. 'I'll nip off home now and get a meal. Mind you're ready on the doorstep when I get back at half seven.'

Jan was not only ready but she had found time to change into jeans and a chunky white sweater, and undo the ribbon which confined her hair. A few quick swipes with the brush had transformed it into a shining curtain that framed her face and fell just below her shoulders.

Looking into the mirror, she frowned at herself. If only she were tall and slim like Tim's wife, Vanessa, who was a physiotherapist, instead of only five feet two and—in her own opinion—much too rounded. It wasn't that she was overweight—far from it—but it would be nice to be able to flatten out some of her curves, provided it didn't involve a starvation diet.

Jan sighed and shrugged, abandoned the mirror and ran downstairs to the side door of the hospital. Looking out, she spotted Tim just parking his car, and with a wave of her hand she hurried across to the corner where her own was kept.

As she approached the small green MG she hoped devoutly it wouldn't, like Mr Delaney, be in one of its moods. Perhaps it had been a bit mad to buy an open eight-year-old sports car instead of a Mini, or something sensible like that which would be in keeping with her lowly status in the medical world. Truth to tell, it had been an impulse buy, but she had never regretted it, in spite of the car's unreliability. Tearing down the dual carriageway towards the coast with her hair streaming out behind her was very near Jan's idea of heaven.

Today she looked longingly at the hood, neatly in place, but decided against folding it back. There just wasn't time, and it wouldn't be worthwhile anyway for the three-quarter-mile drive to her father's bungalow on the outskirts of Amberwell.

After a frantic search for the key, she unlocked the door and got in. As she switched on the ignition, she found she was holding her breath. The car hadn't behaved too well the last time she had it out. She hoped it was feeling better now.

Her luck was out. The starter whirred ineffectually and the engine remained obstinately silent.

'Come on, love,' she urged the little vehicle. 'Don't mess me about today, *please*!'

But no amount of cajoling had any effect, nor swearing either, though she tried that. If she wasn't going to waste the whole of her precious two hours, she must catch a bus.

Luckily there was a stop just outside the hospital and as she ran down the short drive she could see the vehicle she wanted already stationary, with several people getting off.

Unfortunately there was no one waiting to board it, and as soon as the last person alighted the conductor rang the bell. Thrusting her way through the little crowd of hospital visitors, Jan heard it and leapt forward, her hand outstretched to snatch at the rail. She grabbed it and got one foot on the step, but unfortunately the driver accelerated suddenly before she was able to transfer her weight to jump on.

Faced with a choice between letting go and being dragged along, she relaxed her grip. Even so, she scraped her shin painfully on the edge of the step, momentarily lost her balance and sprawled ignominiously in the gutter.

The people who had alighted noticed nothing—they were already at the entrance to the hospital grounds. But the driver of a silver-grey Mercedes, which had followed Jan slowly from the car park, braked sharply and observed the near-accident with a mixture of exasperation and concern.

The silly girl might have been seriously hurt, and it would serve her right if she had been, doing a daft thing like that. Nevertheless, Adam Delaney supposed he had better stop and ask if she was all right. After all, she had come from the hospital and was probably a nurse who would expect him to recognise her even though she had totally altered her appearance by changing out of uniform.

Ignoring the double yellow line, he stopped by the kerb and got out. Jan was still standing there, wondering what to do. If she waited for another bus it would hardly be worth while visiting her father at all, and yet she had made special arrangements to do so and it was maddening to have them ruined. As she hesitated a voice spoke suddenly from behind her.

'I saw what happened just now and I wondered whether you were all right?' As Jan spun round, flinging her hair back from her face, Adam Delaney started and continued in astonishment, 'Good heavens—it's Dr Latham! What on earth were you thinking of to take a stupid risk like that?'

'I'd have been all right if the bus hadn't accelerated just then.'

'I daresay, but I still think it was a daft thing to do.' His voice softened. 'I don't want my team decimated by the house surgeon turning herself into a patient.'

'I didn't have time to think,' she told him, tilting her chin defiantly. 'I badly needed to catch that bus.'

Adam looked at her thoughtfully. 'Were you going far?'

'Only to see my father. It's no distance at all, but I haven't got much time. Tim is only covering for me until half past nine and I don't want to be late back.'

'Would it help if I gave you a lift?'

Her obvious astonishment was not flattering, but the eagerness with which she accepted the offer made him glad he had made it. He opened the door for her and stood holding it like a chauffeur, but just as Jan was about to get in, she paused and glanced at the delicate upholstery.

'I don't think I'd better—I'm rather muddy——'

'Not to worry. The mud's only on the front of your jeans and you aren't going to sit on that part, so hop in and don't argue or you'll waste even more of your precious time. Where do you want to go?'

She gave him the address and sat back comfortably, prepared to enjoy this unexpected trip in a super car. After a moment Adam asked if she didn't have a car of her own.

'Oh yes, but it wouldn't start.' She hesitated and then added honestly, 'I'm afraid it might be my fault. It's rather old, you see, and doesn't get the attention it should.'

'It never pays to neglect an old car. What is yours? A Mini?'

'No, it's not! It's that green MG parked in the far corner of the car park. You've probably never noticed it——'

'Indeed I have!' Adam turned towards her, his face alight with interest. 'I wondered who was the lucky owner of that car. If I weren't a consultant, obliged to keep up appearances, I'd have some sort of sports car, and I wouldn't mind how old it was either. I enjoy tinkering with engines.'

'Like you enjoy tinkering with hearts,' Jan said. 'On the operating table, I mean,' she added hastily, thinking of all the nurses who imagined themselves in love with him.

Adam made no reply. He was slowing down and a moment later he swung the big car off the main road they had been following, and turned into a quiet tree-lined avenue where the detached houses looked as though they had been there for some time.

'It's nice around here,' he said appreciatively. 'I sometimes wish my flat wasn't right in the town centre, but it's handy to have it over my consulting-rooms.'

'I'm afraid we don't live in such an elegant road as this,' Jan told him. 'Our turning is the second

on this side and it's all bungalows. My father has
to spend most of his time in a wheelchair and——'

'He's a paraplegic?'

'Not exactly, but he had a serious car crash some
years ago and can only walk with great difficulty.'

'That was bad luck.'

'Yes.' Jan clamped her teeth tightly on the
monosyllable and hoped he wouldn't want to
know any more. Even after all this time she
didn't like talking about that awful accident
which had left her motherless and wrecked her
father's life.

Considerably less insensitive than she
imagined, Adam had no intention of probing, and
at that moment she startled him by giving a small
shriek of horror.

She was staring down at her right foot where a
slowly spreading bright red stain was threatening
the pale grey carpet. Frantically she groped in her
pocket for a handkerchief. Mr Delaney would
never forgive her if she left a bloodstain in his
lovely car. And after he'd been kind enough to
give her a lift too!

'There's a box of tissues on the shelf in front of
you,' he said calmly as she still struggled in the
tight jeans.

'Oh, thanks.' Jan snatched at the container and
pulled out enough to mop up a whole pool of
blood.

'I thought you said you weren't hurt,' he
remarked when she had dealt with the situation.

'I knew I'd scraped my shin, but I thought my

jeans would have protected me from a bad graze. I suppose it's been quietly bleeding all the time we've been driving along.'

'When you get to your home you must attend to it at once.' On the verge of giving her precise instructions, he reminded himself she was also a doctor. 'Are your anti-tetanus jabs up to date?' he asked instead.

Jan assured him they were and leaned forward, pointing ahead. 'That's our bungalow over there, the one with the boat in the front garden.'

A small neat board announced that the bungalow was called The Moorings, an appropriate name in view of the large dark blue and cream boat, supported by a cradle, which occupied most of the front lawn. Adam stared at it in amazement. Surely it didn't belong to her father? An almost crippled man couldn't possibly cope with a sailing vessel. For one thing, he would find it extremely difficult even to get on board.

And then he noticed the scaffolding on the far side, offering a comparatively easy ascent from the ground level to the deck—easy, that was, for anyone with normal use of his legs. Could a man who spent most of his time in a wheelchair climb up there?

Knowledgeable about boats himself, Adam longed to ask questions, but restrained himself. Jan already had her hand on the door handle, preparatory to getting out.

'I'm terribly grateful, Mr Delaney,' she began,

then broke off in consternation.

A wheelchair, empty and forlorn-looking, was tilted backwards into a bed of red-and-yellow tulips halfway up the sloping drive. Of the owner there was no sign at all.

CHAPTER TWO

ON THE VERGE of driving away, Adam also noticed the wheelchair and got out of his car instead. Jan was staring about her in a distracted sort of way, and he quickly joined her.

'I can't think where my father is. He can only walk a short distance.' She went across to the wheelchair and righted it. 'He can't be very far away.'

As he spoke an indignant voice from above their heads startled them both.

'Thank God somebody's turned up at last! I've been marooned up here over an hour—all my own fault too.'

A middle-aged man with a thick mass of white hair had emerged from the boat's tiny cabin and now stood holding on to the rail of the cockpit and looking down at them.

'Dad!' Relief showed plainly in Jan's face and voice. 'I couldn't think what had happened to you. How on earth did your chair get in the flowerbed?'

'I forgot to put the brake on, didn't I, and it was away before I'd got to t e top of the scaffolding. Daft thing to do, and after all these years too. You'd think I would have learned to be more careful!'

He began to move very slowly to the side of the boat and Adam saw he had calipers on both legs. Without their help, no doubt, he wouldn't be able to walk at all.

Jan pushed the chair across to the bottom of the scaffolding and manoeuvred it carefully into position. When she had put the brake on, she turned her back and rejoined Adam.

'I can't bear to watch him coming down,' she said in a low voice. 'I think I'll go indoors and put the kettle on or something.'

'And I must be on my way.'

'It was so kind of you to give me a lift. Er—won't you stay and have some coffee or——'

'I don't know what you two are whispering about down there,' came an irate voice from above. 'Isn't it about time you introduced me to your friend, Janice?'

'He's not my friend—he's my boss.' Noticing Adam's lifted brows. Jan paused to laugh at herself. 'This is Mr Delaney.'

'Glad to meet you, Mr Latham,' Adam began.

'Don't elevate me to the ranks of surgery, Mr Delaney. I'm Dr Latham, GP.'

'I'm sorry—I'm afraid I didn't know you were in the same profession as your daughter.'

'I still practise too, even though it's only part-time.' Robert Latham arrived painfully on the bottom level of the scaffolding and began to transfer himself to the wheelchair. 'Going to be confusing, having two Dr Lathams in the house—that is, if you're staying for a drink, and I hope you are. Why don't you call my daughter by her christian name—Janice?'

'Nobody uses my full name except you, Dad,' she protested. Without looking at Adam, she said diffidently, 'Most people call me Jan, and I much prefer that.'

The charming smile which captivated the patients shone out for a moment. 'OK then—Jan it shall be.'

'I hope that means you'll join me in a drink.' Robert steered his chair past a car parked just outside the garage and began to propel himself towards the front door. 'Personally I could use a good strong drink—whisky for preference. How about you?'

'It would suit me very well, but not too strong, please, since I'm driving.' Pausing while his host led the way up a ramp and into the hall, Adam glanced back over his shoulder. 'You've got a magnificent boat there.'

'*Sea Lady*'s not bad, not bad at all. Know anything about boats?'

'A little. I had a sailing dinghy when I was a schoolboy, but I've never actually owned a boat since then, though I sometimes crew for friends.'

'Any time you want a sail during the summer, just give me a ring. I've got a couple of regulars who help me, but I don't care to call on them too often. Their wives are apt to kick up a fuss.' Robert whirled his chair round. 'Can't manage sails myself now, unfortunately, but I still take the helm.'

They entered a long room which overlooked the front garden and, at the other end, had french windows giving a view of lawn and flower beds, all very neat and colourful but somehow looking as though tended by someone more used to a public park.

Which was probably the case, Adam reflected. Even someone as resourceful as Dr Latham would surely find gardening impossible. It was clear that he managed to maintain his boat, though, since his ancient tweed jacket was paint-stained and a strong smell of white spirit emanated from him.

'What will you have, Janice?' her father asked, moving towards a loaded drinks table. 'Sherry?'

'Yes, please.' A sore feeling halfway down her right leg reminded her of her promise to her boss. 'But I'll go and—er—wash my hands first. I had a bit of trouble with the car—that's why Mr Delaney was giving me a lift.'

The two men resumed their conversation about boats and neither appeared to notice her departure. In the bathroom she rolled up her jeans and dealt conscientiously with a large raw patch which was still oozing blood.

As she tidied away the materials she had been using, she was assailed by a strong sense of unreality. She had only been back in her home town three weeks and during that time she couldn't really feel she had advanced at all in her relationship with Adam Delaney. Nor had she expected to. He was a consultant, a being far above her, someone whom she called 'sir' who had the right to make her look a fool if she didn't reach the high standard he required of his house surgeon. Like this morning, for instance.

And yet here he was in her father's sitting-room, drinking whisky and talking about boats. It was incredible and obviously a one-off occasion which would never happen again.

Her return was as unobtrusive as her exit had been and she made no attempt to join in the conversation, nor did either of the men try to draw her in. As she sipped her sherry she glanced at the clock. Time was flying and she would soon have to leave if she wasn't going to be late back. It was a relief when Adam put down his glass and stood up.

'Thanks a lot, Dr Latham. That was a remarkably fine whisky.'

'The best malt. Some of the stuff they put in bottles these days isn't worth drinking.' Robert waved a nonchalant hand. 'Don't forget that phone call if you fancy a sail. *Sea Lady* will be going in the water in, say, a couple of weeks, so any time after that, weather permitting, just give me a ring.'

Jan went with Adam to the front door, thanked him again for coming to her rescue, and watched him striding down the drive. He hadn't called her 'Jan' after all and she didn't imagine he ever would now. Even if he took her father up on his offer of a sail, it was most unlikely she would be present.

'How are you, Dad?' she asked as she returned to the sitting-room and sat down.

It was at once apparent she had said the wrong thing. Robert frowned and twitched his shoulders irritably.

'I never know what to say when people ask me that. I could, of course, reply, "Fine!" which seems to be the general custom nowadays regardless of the person's state of health. Or I could say mournfully, "As well as can be expected," which is definitely not my style. I suppose the best reply is that I'm exactly as I was a week ago, when you saw me last. Will that do?'

'It will do very well,' Jan said equably. 'Is there anything you want me to do now I'm here?'

'Nothing that Mrs Jackson can't attend to in the morning.' Her father's voice warmed. 'She really is a splendid woman—miles better than any of the other daily housekeepers I've had since my accident. Talks too much, of course, but there's always something.' He shot a keen look at his daughter. 'You're looking tired, Janice, but I suppose that's only to be expected. I remember when I was a houseman I felt like death warmed up most of the time.'

'I didn't get much sleep last night.'

'You ought to be getting used to that by now, though I suppose it's harder for the young to do without sleep than it is for old 'uns like me. How many more houseman jobs do you want to take before you feel ready for general practice?'

'I thought another couple.' Jan tried to imagine

herself in general practice and failed completely. It wasn't that the idea was new to her. She had been destined to join her father's partners ever since she took up medicine, but somehow her future had narrowed since she qualified. Getting through each day—worrying, even frightening, but always interesting—had become of paramount importance and she looked no farther than the next twenty-four hours, or perhaps a precious free weekend.

It would all be quite different when she became a community doctor. She would get to know people, whole families of them, be responsible for treating their aches and pains, getting the blame if she diagnosed wrongly. Terrifying!

'Two ought to be enough,' her father was saying. 'It'll be a great day for me when your name is added to the list of doctors on the board outside the surgery. It's something I've dreamt about. After all, it's *our* family practice, started and built up by your grandfather between the wars. You'll be the third Dr Latham.'

Jan, to whom words came so easily—sometimes too easily—could think of nothing to say. Fortunately her father didn't seem to be expecting an answer. He was looking at his watch and changing the subject.

'How are you getting back to the hospital?'

'By bus, I expect, if I'm lucky, but I'm afraid I ought to be going now in case I have to walk. Tim is covering for me and I don't want to be late.'

Robert had been about to pour himself another drink, but he put the bottle down again. 'I'll drive you. I'm not entirely useless, you know.'

'I never supposed you were.' She gave him an affectionate smile and leaned back in her chair. 'Now I can stay another fifteen minutes.'

The time melted away like magic, and soon she was seated beside her father in the big old-fashioned car which had been converted to hand controls. He backed it expertly out of the drive, leaving his wheelchair awaiting his return, and drove briskly out of the residential area and along the straight road leading into the town. Here a tangle of one-way streets awaited them, but both were familiar with the maze and found it tiresome but not intimidating. Within a few minutes they reached a quieter district and the hospital appeared at the top of a slight rise.

Like most hospitals of its period, Amberwell had been added to many times, but somehow the conglomeration had managed to retain a reasonably symmetrical shape which accorded well with the imposing main entrance with its pillars and stone canopy.

'Thanks a lot, Dad. I'll see you again soon.' Jan opened the door and jumped out.

'I'll be delighted to have a visit from you any time you can manage to fit one in—so long as you don't feel you've got to keep tabs on me,' Robert called after her, but she was already out of earshot.

Jan had expected to find Tim in the doctors'

sitting-room, but the only person there was
Louise Norton, a pretty girl with dark curly hair,
who was house surgeon to the RSO.

'Have you seen Tim?' asked Jan, hovering in
the doorway.

'He was here not long ago, but then he got an
emergency call from the Unit and went dashing
off.'

'I suppose I'd better go and look for him there,
then. He's covering for me and he'll want to get
off home.'

Not bothering to use the lift, Jan went swiftly
downstairs to the ground floor and through a
connecting door leading to the Accident and
Emergency Unit. This was the newest part of the
hospital and had been built out at the back, with
its own entrance on what had once been a quiet
road.

There were a few people waiting either
anxiously or apathetically on the scarlet chairs,
but otherwise the place seemed deserted except
for the girl at the desk.

As Jan hesitated a nurse came out from behind
the drawn curtains of a cubicle and looked at her
enquiringly.

'Dr Robertson,' Jan said. 'I was told he was
here.'

'Yes, he is. We had a bad heart case brought in
and the Casualty Officer sent for him.' The nurse
jerked her head. 'He's in that cubicle.'

For a moment Jan's first sensation was of relief
because she hadn't been the doctor who had had to

cope with a bad case from scratch. She *knew* what to do, of course, but she hadn't yet acquired the necessary confidence. Nevertheless, she would probably have to handle the patient on her own from now on, so the sooner she got clued up the better.

As she approached the drawn curtains, from behind which came a low murmur of voices, she had absolutely no premonition of the shock in store for her.

The little cubicle seemed full of people, but at first she could only see Tim's back view as he bent over someone on the examination couch, and the Casualty Officer standing next to him. There was a staff nurse there as well, and another person on the far side.

Then, as she squeezed herself in on Tim's other side, she saw that the hitherto invisible member of the party was Peter Felgate.

The charge nurse should have gone off duty at eight o'clock, though it was true that he sometimes had to stay late. What was really unusual was for him to be here in the Unit. He was looking so worried too, his rugged face full of distress.

Jan's gaze dropped to the patient round whom they were all standing. It was a woman of about fifty, blue-lipped and deathly pale, with beads of sweat on her forehead and upper lip. She was deeply unconscious and her breathing was noisy and fast. In mounting horror, Jan recognised her as Peter's mother.

She had known Margaret Felgate most of her life and had always been fond of her, even regarding her sometimes as a surrogate mother. It was shattering to see her like this.

Tim turned round, his face expressionless. 'I've got a new patient for you, Jan,' he said quietly. 'Perhaps you'll make the necessary arrangements for admittance while I finish writing her notes.'

It was not possible, then, to say anything to Peter. Jan flung him a glance which she tried to make full of sympathy, noted with pain the anguish in his eyes, and went out again to get busy on the phone. One of the two side wards on Nightingale was empty, she remembered, and Mrs Felgate had better be put in there.

Within a few minutes Tim had handed over responsibility to her and gone home, and she was walking beside the trolley with Peter on the other side. Neither of them spoke. While the porter was with them there was nothing that could be said.

Staff Nurse Kennedy, a married part-timer who was in charge of Peter's two wards at night three times a week, was looking out for them while her junior put the finishing touches to the side ward. She was a quiet woman who kept her emotions strictly under control, and she said only, 'We're all ready for her, Peter,' and held the door wide for the trolley to pass.

'I expect you'd like to stay for a while,' she said to Peter when his mother had been carefully transferred to the special heart bed.

He spoke for the first time. 'Yes, of course, Staff.' A faint bleak smile briefly lightened his grim expression. 'It'll save you having to keep a watch on the side ward in addition to your other duties.'

She nodded, hiding her relief with lowered lashes. 'Shall I take the notes now, doctor?' she said to Jan, holding out her hand.

'I haven't had time to read them yet, so I'll hang on to them for a bit.' Jan withdrew slightly from the group by the bed and began to read.

Nothing that she saw written in Tim's spidery writing made her feel any happier about the situation. Out of a mass of medical detail she gathered that the heart attack had been really severe and the next twenty-four hours would be of vital importance. She longed to ask what had actually happened and whether Peter had been present. As she struggled to frame her question he told her all about it.

'I left here in good time and went straight home. She was getting supper ready and she turned round to greet me—and collapsed. Just like that.'

'What an absolutely terrible shock!' Jan's voice was soft with sympathy. 'It was totally unexpected, wasn't it?'

'It certainly was by me, and I don't think she had any suspicions herself either.' His tone indicated the depth of his bitterness. 'Just think, Jan—I shared a house with her and never guessed her heart was bad. How *could* I have been so blind? You'd have thought it would have been obvious, specially to anyone who reckoned to know something about hearts.'

'You know as well as I do it isn't always so obvious. Your mother's a bit overweight and if she ever seemed rather breathless you'd put it down to that. You mustn't blame yourself for not noticing.'

'I *do* blame myself and I always shall. You'd be the same if it was your father.'

Jan sighed. He was right, of course, and there was nothing she could say which would help him in his distress.

They stood by the bed in silence for a moment and then Peter glanced down at her. 'Oughtn't you to be making your late round?'

She roused herself. 'Yes, I must get on with it, but I'll be back, Peter. I expect you'll be staying for quite a while.'

'All night,' he said briefly.

'You can't do that! You've got to work tomorrow.'

Across the bed his eyes challenged her. 'Do you really think I could go home and leave her like this? Anything could happen in the night—you know that.'

Jan knew only too well, and she knew, too, how Peter felt about his mother. He had, in a way, taken the place of the father who had, long ago, gone off with another woman. He had dealt with bureaucracy on his mother's behalf, sorted out her finances and been her friend as well as her son. Not that Margaret was a helpless type of woman, but she was old-fashioned and preferred to concentrate on running the home while her man looked after outside matters.

Without attempting to argue further, Jan left the side ward and started her round. Adam had several patients in the private ward at the far end of the hospital, and she went there first, making sure that everyone was comfortable and ready to settle down for the night. Back in Simpson and Nightingale, she found a few problems, but nothing serious. After that, all her duties faithfully performed, she could spend a little time with Peter.

He was sitting by the bed, the shaded lamp turning his light brown hair to gold. He had been leaning forward, his eyes on his mother's unconscious face, but he looked up as Jan came in and rose restlessly to his feet.

'Any change?' she asked.

He shook his head and, acting impulsively, she went to him and slipped her arm through his. Closely linked, they stood looking down at the patient.

It seemed impossible that this was the kindly neighbour who had done so much to help Jan through the traumatic experience of losing her own mother when she was only fifteen and having her other parent in hospital for weeks. After they moved to the bungalow she didn't see so much of Mrs Felgate, but she retained a firm affection for her and could guess how Peter must be feeling.

'People often make a wonderful recovery after a bad heart attack these days,' she said quietly. 'There hasn't been much time for the medication to take effect.'

'I do have some medical knowledge,' he snapped at her. 'Even though I'm not a doctor.'

Jan was hurt and showed it, though she understood it was his pain which had caused him to lash out at her.

'I'm sorry, love.' He had noticed her expression, though she said nothing. Slipping his arm out of her grasp, he put it round her shoulders and turned her to face him.

Instinctively, Jan lifted her face. They had kissed often enough in the past, though not so much recently as when they were younger. It seemed the most natural thing in the world for her to offer her mouth, and Peter accepted the gesture naturally.

His other arm came round her and for a moment he laid his cheek against hers as she held him close in the only gesture of comfort she knew how to make.

Neither of them noticed that the door, which Jan had left ajar, was being pushed wider. Adam Delaney even stood for a moment looking at them in astonishment before they became aware of his presence and sprang apart as guiltily as though they had been caught in a much more compromising situation than the one he had interrupted.

'So sorry to disturb you.' His voice was icy. 'I understand that I have a new patient in this ward.'

CHAPTER THREE

ADAM had returned to the hospital to take another look at one of his cases in the children's ward, a baby who was to have a hole-in-the-heart repair job in the morning. He had not been quite satisfied with the child's condition when he had visited her earlier, and a fresh inspection caused him to decide to wait a little longer.

It was a chance meeting with the Casualty Officer which informed him he had a new patient in Nightingale, Charge Nurse Felgate's mother.

'Might as well go along,' said Adam, 'seeing that I'm on the premises.' It would also be an opportunity to check on Caroline Garnham, about whom he was seriously worried.

He had expected to find Peter with his mother. What he didn't expect was to find his house surgeon clasped in the charge nurse's arms.

The expression on their faces when he appeared so suddenly would have been laughable if he hadn't found the situation extremely annoying. After all, a consultant had a right to expect the most junior member of his team to attend to duty and not to indulge in amorous embraces when actually on the ward.

They sprang apart, Jan's fair skin suffused with colour. She seemed totally speechless, but Peter said stiffly, 'This is my mother, sir. She had a cardiac arrest earlier this evening.'

'So I understand.' Adam did not trouble to explain how he knew. 'May I see the chart, please?'

Jan, who was nearest, unclipped it from the bottom of the bed and handed it over. Her cheeks were still burning and she felt an utter fool—and not for the first time that day either. Mr Delaney's already poor opinion of her would be even worse now, but to try and explain how the embrace had come about would only make matters worse.

He read the few entries carefully and then put his fingers on the limp wrist as he studied the patient intently.

'She's holding her own,' he said abruptly. 'Holding it very well indeed. There should be some improvement before long.'

'I hope so, sir.' Peter's voice shook a little.

Adam looked at him thoughtfully, noting the lines of strain. To have a shock like that on top of a long day's work must have been devastating.

'If you're intending to remain here all night,' he went on, 'you'd better try and get some sleep.' His ironic glance shifted to Jan. 'I'm sure my house surgeon will be able to fix up something for you in the way of bedding before she goes off duty.'

'I expect so,' Jan said woodenly.

A twinkle appeared in Adam's brilliant eyes. 'Don't make him too comfortable,' he warned, and left the room with a chuckle on his way to see if Caroline was sleeping peacefully.

As soon as he could be presumed to be out of earshot, Jan burst into agitated speech. 'I've never been so embarrassed in my life! What must he have thought?'

'That we know each other rather well, that's all. Anyway, what's it matter what he thought?'

'Don't be daft, Peter, of course it matters!'

'Well, I suppose it might a little,' he conceded, 'but your private life is your own affair.'

'It would be if I had any, but I'm nearly always here, and that means I can't please myself what I do.'

He looked at his watch. 'Actually you're not on duty now, only on call, and that's a different thing altogether.'

'No, it isn't.'

They continued to argue, although Jan felt privately they had flogged the subject to death, and she was only keeping it going because Peter seemed to have shed a little of his tension. Perhaps the visit of Adam Delaney had something to do with that and she ought to be glad he had turned up instead of making such a fuss.

'I'll go and see about your bed,' she said eventually.

'There's no need for you to bother——'

'I had my instructions, remember?'

Staff Nurse Kennedy was sympathetic and very willing to provide blankets and a pillow. 'There's an empty bed just inside Simpson. The poor young chap can lie down there and perhaps get some sleep. Is he the only one available to take care of his mum?'

Jan nodded. 'His father left her years ago and he hasn't any brothers or sisters. I used to live next door when I was at school and he was always very close to her then.'

'It's nice when you get a relationship like that, though I sometimes wonder, when it's a son who's so devoted, whether it prevents him marrying. Some mothers on their own can get very jealous of a daughter-in-law.'

'I don't think Mrs Felgate would be like that. I never saw any sign of it.'

'Well, I don't suppose you would, dear, not unless you were thinking of marrying Charge Nurse Felgate yourself.'

Jan shrugged and made no reply. She was suddenly so tired she felt she would fall asleep standing up if she didn't get to bed within the next few minutes.

'Goodnight, Staff,' she said abruptly. 'If I get called out tonight I won't be answerable for the consequences.'

Her luck was in and she slept soundly for nearly seven hours. When the alarm clock shrilled its noisy warning, her first thought was for Mrs Felgate, and she resolved to go along to

Nightingale as soon as she had showered and dressed.

At that hour of the morning the ward was a hive of activity with nurses whisking past the nurses' station in all directions. But in the small side ward all was quiet. At a casual glance it looked as though nothing had changed. Peter was still there, now much in need of a shave, and the patient seemed just the same too.

Jan went straight up to the bed and picked up the chart, which had been carefully kept all through the night. At once she noted an improvement, and as she put her fingers on the pulse Margaret Felgate opened her eyes.

'Jan——' Her voice was very weak but clear. 'Where am I? What's happened?'

Before Jan could answer Peter was at the bedside. 'You had a funny turn, Mum, and now you're in hospital, but don't worry—you're much better this morning.'

'I wondered why Jan was in a white coat. You look very professional, dear.'

Jan smiled, appreciating the compliment even in those circumstances. 'Don't try to talk too much, Mrs Felgate. Just rest quietly and leave everything to the nurses.'

The patient, who still seemed utterly exhausted, closed her eyes obediently and Jan withdrew slightly from the bed.

'What sort of night did you have?' she asked Peter in a low tone. 'Did you get any sleep?'

'Enough to keep me going. Actually, Mum

came round about three a.m., but she didn't realise where she was and drifted into natural sleep, which was the best thing for her.' He rubbed his hand over his chin. 'I'd better nip off home and make myself look presentable for the day.' Formally, he added, 'You think it would be OK for me to do that, Jan?'

Realising he was asking for her professional opinion, Jan answered in the same tone and did not show the slight embarrassment his question had caused her. Peter had been nursing heart cases for three years and probably knew much more about them than she did.

'Just tell one of the staff nurses you're going,' she advised. 'Don't forget to have some breakfast.'

When he had gone she remembered her own need for food and went along to the canteen. Louise Norton was there, sipping a cup of coffee, and she eyed Jan's loaded plate with disgust.

'I really don't know how you can!'

'If I tried to get through the morning on an apple and a cup of coffee, like you, I'd collapse at Adam Delaney's feet—and you can guess what he'd think of that!'

Louise smiled, her dark eyes dancing. 'No problem! Do you like working with the great man now you've had three weeks of it?'

Jan paused with a loaded fork halfway to her mouth. Did she like working with Mr Delaney? Louise would think her daft if she admitted she didn't know. There were times when she liked it very much, but other times she seethed under his scarcely veiled contempt.

'I feel I'm learning a lot from him,' she began cautiously, only to be interrupted.

'What's that supposed to mean? He has quite a reputation with women, you know.'

Jan had known that the nurses tended to fall for him in a big way, but since coming to Amberwell she had concentrated so hard on the professional side of her life that she had scarcely even wondered whether her boss might have other activities. Until yesterday, that was, when he had revealed himself as surprisingly human and interested in boats.

Louise was waiting for an answer and she hastily produced one. 'Do you speak from personal experience?'

'Partly. I went out with Adam once or twice when I first came here. He's very attractive—I admit that—but not really my type. Besides, I discovered he was dating that pretty Sister in the Orthopaedic Department as well, and I don't much care for sharing my men. One really should be able to count on undivided attention for the brief while an affair lasts. Don't you agree?'

'Perhaps he felt there was safety in numbers?' Jan suggested.

'What a horrible expression that is!' Louise wrinkled her shapely nose. 'There's no such thing as safety where men and women are concerned, so watch it, my love. I have a feeling that innocent expression of yours might just possibly be genuine.'

Innocent expression! Left alone, Jan sat fuming over the last of her breakfast. She hadn't been regarded as particularly innocent in her student days, but since then she had always been too busy for dalliance with the opposite sex. And after she had come back to Amberwell there was always Peter in the background. If ever she needed an escort she could call on him.

Breakfast over, she did a quick tour of the hospital, checking on Adam's operation cases. He would start about nine-thirty and she wanted to have up-to-date information about each of them in case he should ask for it.

In the children's ward she was surprised to find little Marilyn Masters being given a drink of orange juice.

'That child's for operation this morning!' she said sharply. 'Why on earth are you giving her a drink? Mr Delaney will be furious and she'll have to be postponed.'

The young student looked at her in surprise. 'Marilyn's been taken off the list. Didn't you know?'

'No, I didn't! When did this happen?'

'Last evening. Mr Delaney came to the hospital late. I wasn't on duty, of course, but it said in the night report that Marilyn's op had been put off because she's got a slight cold. Didn't he tell you?'

'Obviously not,' snapped Jan, taking out her indignation on the student nurse, who couldn't really be blamed for anything except irritatingly unnecessary questions.

Why on earth hadn't Adam mentioned he'd been to the children's ward when he paid his unfortunate visit to Mrs Felgate? He shouldn't keep his house surgeon in the dark about patients. It wasn't fair!

Or was his reticence, perhaps, due to the fact that he was so disgusted at the situation in which he had found Peter and herself that he didn't feel like taking her into his confidence about anything at all?

'I wish you'd told me about Marilyn being taken off the list, sir,' she said when they met in the theatre ante-room. 'I felt an awful fool telling a nurse off for giving a drink.'

Adam looked down at her calmly. He was standing in singlet and trousers preparatory to donning theatre garb. A dark mat of hair showed plainly above the white garment and his bare arms looked strong and muscular.

'It was a last-minute decision,' he said carelessly.

Jan opened her mouth to remind him that he'd known about it the previous evening, and then closed it again. The less said about last night the better!

Tim came in and began to bustle about getting ready, talking cheerfully as he did so. Jan made no attempt to join in their masculine conversation. There were times when she felt very much the odd one out. She was so very far behind the two men in surgical experience. Only time could alter that situation and raise her to the level of a junior registrar.

Junior registrar? What on earth was she thinking of! She'd never be a registrar on a cardiac team or any other. She was going into general practice.

Their first case was the most difficult and delicate repair job which Jan had seen so far. The heart was young—it belonged to a woman in her twenties—but it had been diseased for a long time and needed all Adam's skill. The operation took the whole morning, and when it had been successfully concluded and the patient wheeled off to the recovery-room, the entire team relaxed in a glow of mutual content.

'Very tricky,' said Tim, peeling off his gloves. 'You did a marvellous job, if you don't mind me saying so, sir.'

Adam was in a good mood, the irritability he had displayed the previous day all forgotten. But in the midst of his satisfaction he thought suddenly of Caroline. If only her heart could be mended as this one had been. If only he didn't have to send her home in a few days, slightly improved by rest and treatment but with so little hope for the future.

He thrust the thought to the back of his mind and concentrated instead on his successful morning. Consequently, his good mood lasted all day, and Jan, observing it and feeling thankful, hoped it would go on for ever.

That was obviously too much to expect, but she did have a whole week of comparative peace, a week during which Peter's mother made steady if slow progress and none of Adam's other patients gave cause for alarm. Then it was operating day again, with a fairly routine list which presented no special difficulties, except that the morning took longer than expected so that they were late breaking for lunch.

As Jan pulled off the hideous cap which covered all her bright hair, the telephone rang. Since she was the nearest she lifted the receiver.

'Theatre ante-room. Dr Latham speaking.'

'Is Mr Delaney there?' came the voice of the switchboard girl. And when Jan confirmed it, she continued in an agitated sort of way quite unlike her usual bored tones, 'Thank goodness for that! Will you tell him I've got a call for him, please? She's been ringing off and on all the morning and nearly driving me crazy. I told her he was operating, but she actually seemed to want me to call him out to the phone, if you ever heard of such a thing. It would have been more than my life was worth!'

The girl was evidently in a hurry to get rid of her troublesome caller, for she switched the call through before Jan had time to put the receiver down and summon Adam to the phone.

'Julie here.' A high-pitched, slightly hysterical voice came on the line. 'I've been trying to get you for *ages*, but that girl was terribly unhelpful—said you were operating and couldn't be disturbed. I'm sure you'd have come to the phone if you'd known it was *me.*'

Jan seized her opportunity to break in as the voice paused for breath. 'I'll get Mr Delaney for you.'

'You're not Adam? Why ever didn't you say so before?'

Resisting the temptation to say, 'You didn't give me a chance,' Jan laid down the receiver while the caller was still complaining and went to summon Adam.

He had been enjoying a joke with Tim and was feeling cheerful and relaxed. He crossed the room still laughing and picked up the receiver, and immediately his face changed.

'What do you want, Julie?' he demanded curtly as soon as she announced her identity.

'It's my car. Honestly, Adam, it's given nothing but trouble ever since you bought it for me. And the garage isn't a bit helpful—they keep on saying there's nothing wrong with it and I just *know* there is. It conked out at some traffic lights the other day and I couldn't re-start it. Some men had to push me out of the way, and I felt most dreadfully humiliated.'

'I presume you got it going eventually?'

'One of the men did it for me. He said I'd choked it, but I'm sure I hadn't.'

'Knowing you, I should think he was probably right.'

'Don't be so mean! I'm a very good driver.'

'That's open to question,' Adam said grimly.

'I've never had an accident—well, not a proper accident, just one or two incidents, so there!' Julie waited a moment, apparently expecting he would continue the argument, but as Adam remained silent she went on speaking. 'So what are you going to do about it?'

'I suppose I'd better take a look at the car, just to satisfy you, but I'm not sure when I can manage it. I'll give you a ring within the next day or so.'

'That's no good! I thought you'd do it today. *Please*, Adam, don't leave me stranded without a reliable car!'

'I'm not leaving you stranded. There's absolutely no reason why you shouldn't use the car—but do try not to choke it. Engines don't like that sort of treatment.' He banged down the receiver and turned away, scowling.

The others had been changing into ordinary clothes with a view to getting some lunch. No one had taken much notice of Adam's conversation, but he was so obviously put out by it that there was a sudden and slightly uncomfortable silence. It only lasted a moment and then Jan broke it.

'What time do you want to re-start, sir?'

Adam considered, still frowning, and then ordered them to be back at half-past two. A quick peep at her watch told Jan she had thirty-five minutes for lunch, which ought to be enough even for her healthy appetite.

In the canteen she found Louise Norton, just finishing her own meal. 'Hi!' Jan unloaded her tray and sat down opposite.

Louise responded automatically, her eyes wide and thoughtful.

'Anything wrong?' asked Jan, beginning on her ploughman's.

'We just lost a patient.'

'Expected?'

Louise shrugged. 'Yes and no. It was a toss-up, but we all hoped it wouldn't happen. Talk to me, Jan, and take my mind off it.'

'Do you know who Julie is?' Jan asked, saying the first thing which came into her head.

'Julie? It's an ordinary sort of name and doesn't ring any particular bell at the moment. Can't you give me a clue?'

'Adam Delaney was talking to her on the phone. I got the impression he knew her rather well.'

To her surprise Louise's unhappy expression was replaced by a smile. 'I should say he does know her well! She's his wife.' She glanced at the clock above the counter and jumped to her feet. 'My God, is that the time? I must fly—see you!'

Jan nodded and went on eating her lunch, giving no sign of the surprise she had just received.

And yet why should it have been such a shock to discover her boss was married? Certainly he had given no appearance of being a married man—hadn't Louise mentioned a number of brief affairs with various members of hospital staff? A moment's thought was sufficient to convince her she was being extraordinarily naïve to imagine a wife in the background would necessarily make any difference to that sort of thing. Particularly with a man like Adam.

Or was she misjudging him?

CHAPTER FOUR

JAN finished her lunch at record speed and found herself with ten minutes to spare. Should she put her feet up in the doctors' sitting-room or go outside for a breath of fresh air? Choosing the latter, she turned towards the entrance hall, where the revolving doors showed her a pleasantly sunlit scene. They received her into their circle of almost perpetual motion and swept her out into a different world.

She sat down on a low wall and lifted her face to the warmth. Immediately her conversation with Louise drifted back to her mind. Somehow she hadn't thought that Adam Delaney was married, and yet—why not? He was far too attractive a man not to have been snatched up by some female.

Jan's eyes were closing and she jerked herself wide awake. Time to go in. On the way back to resume work she again met Louise, whisking along a corridor with her white jacket flying open and her stethoscope dangling.

'I forgot to tell you Vanessa Robertson was looking for you this morning.' She paused momentarily.

'You'd think, being Tim's wife, she'd have remembered it's operating day,' Jan said.

'She's probably too immersed in her physiotherapy work to think about her husband's commitments. Anyway, she wants you to go to a party—on Friday week. 'Bye for now!'

Interested but not very hopeful of being able to go, Jan went on to the theatre to get ready for the afternoon list. Scrubbing up, she sensed Adam was now in one of his moods, though he had been all right during the morning, and she had better watch it!

Fortunately, the afternoon list was worked through without incident and there were no explosions, but as they were leaving the ante-room afterwards he detained her for a moment.

'Have you had that car seen to yet?'

Jan gave a guilty start. She'd meant to book it in to the local garage before she started work that morning, but there hadn't been time to make the phone call.

'Don't bother to reply,' Adam said sarcastically. 'It's written all over your face that you've done nothing about it. Why not?'

Jan thought of those snatched few minutes out in the sun. She could have made her phone call instead of going outside—if she'd remembered. 'I was afraid of being late getting to theatres,' she prevaricated.

'Am I an ogre, that you apparently daren't take the risk of being late?' he demanded. 'You know as well as I do—or you *should* know—how important it is to keep a car in good running order. You never know when you might need it urgently, and I would have excused you if you'd explained.'

Jan's long gold-tipped lashes quickly veiled the disbelief in her eyes. Not knowing what to say, she kept silent, aware that Adam was hesitating, apparently on the verge of saying something.

Eventually he made up his mind. 'Would you like me to take a look inside the bonnet and find out why it wouldn't start? It's probably only the plugs.'

Her clear skin coloured with a mixture of embarrassment and pleasure. 'It's very kind of you, sir, but do you think you should? Your hands——'

'My hands will come to no harm. I told you I enjoy tinkering with engines.'

'Y—yes, but——'

'Then for goodness' sake stop arguing and give me the keys!'

'I don't bring them to theatres with me,' Jan protested. 'They're in my handbag, and that's locked up in my room.'

'Very well. We'll go up there now and get them.'

She opened her mouth to protest, but thought better of it. But she couldn't help being aware of rumours which would fly round the hospital if anybody saw the heart specialist following her up to her room!

They walked through the wide corridors side by side and eventually came to some narrow stairs which led up to five small rooms occupied by junior doctors on the top floor.

'You live up there?' Adam was amazed. 'It looks like a Victorian servants' quarters. I hope there's a fire escape.'

'Oh yes, of course.' Jan was speeding ahead of him. 'Why don't you wait down below?' she called over her shoulder. 'There's no need to bother to come all the way.'

'But I'm curious. I had no idea there was this secret world tucked away among the attics.' He trudged resolutely behind her and caught her up as she fumbled for the key of her room.

Jan wondered frantically what sort of a state she'd left it in that morning. She couldn't even remember if she'd made her bed, and she was relieved to see the duvet more or less in place. There was an untidy pile of textbooks on the dressing-table and some copies of *The Lancet* on a chair, but no strings of tights dripping over the washbasin, as there might well have been.

Adam crossed to the window and stood staring out at a view of rooftops and chimneys. 'It's peaceful up here,' he commented. 'How many of you live tucked away like this?'

When she told him there were five and the others were all men, he turned round and gave her a long thoughtful stare. 'Do you ever have any trouble with them?'

'Not so far.' Jan tipped out the contents of her bag on the bed. 'I guess we're all too darned tired.'

His brilliant eyes continued to study her. 'I

can't think of any other reason.'

And suddenly the quiet little room was no longer peaceful, and Jan shivered as something like an electric spark flashed between them. Her face was burning and her hands trembled as she sorted through the muddle of odds and ends in her bag. A strange nameless longing possessed her, an emotion so strong that she did not dare even to attempt to name it.

'Here they are!' She snatched up the keys and held them out to him, but as he took them from her the touch of his fingers only added to her confusion. Without a word she turned and led the way out to the corridor.

Adam waited politely at the top of the stairs for her to precede him. She ran quickly down and, reaching the next floor, where there were several wards, looked nervously up and down. At first there was no one in sight, but as he joined her, a nurse came out of one of the wards and stared at them curiously.

The incident obviously made no impact on Adam at all. He said casually, 'I'll let you know how I get on,' and strode away down the corridor.

It was absurd to set off in the opposite direction, but Jan did so all the same, walking in such a trancelike state that she almost collided with Vanessa Robertson on a corner.

'Just the person I wanted to see!' The physiotherapist clutched her by the arm. 'Has Tim told you we're giving a party next Friday to celebrate our fifth wedding anniversary?'

'No, but Louise did——'

'I might have known Tim wouldn't get around to it! He's hopeless at remembering that sort of thing, but men usually are, don't you think?' Tall and blonde, Vanessa smiled down at Jan. 'You will come, won't you?'

'I'd love to,' Jan said warmly, 'but I'm not sure if I can get away.'

'We're quite near the hospital, you know, and we *do* have a phone. You could be on the spot almost as quickly as you could come down from that awful little room of yours. Any time after seven-thirty, and stay as long or as short a time as you like. Right?'

'I'll have to ask the boss——'

'I don't suppose Adam will object. He's going to be there himself.'

Jan could not share Vanessa's confidence. It was more than likely Adam would disapprove of his house surgeon abandoning his patients to enjoy herself at a party, no matter how quickly she could get back. And she wanted to go so very badly, she suddenly discovered. She'd always enjoyed hospital parties and she hadn't been to one since coming to Amberwell.

Her opportunity to ask permission came the next day. She had been visiting the children's ward and they met just outside. She guessed that Adam was also going to pay an informal visit since she knew he held strong views on subjecting his little patients to the ordeal of having a whole team standing round the cot staring at them.

'Morning, Jan!' he greeted her cheerfully.

It was the first time he had used her name, and she was inordinately pleased. It could only mean he was in a good temper and she snatched eagerly at her chance, putting the request as briefly as possible so as not to hold him up unnecessarily. 'You don't mind if I go to the party, since the Robertsons live so near to the hospital?' she finished anxiously.

Adam looked down at her, meeting the pleading hazel-green eyes with a smile dawning in his own. She was like a child begging for a treat and he was conscious of an odd sort of tenderness towards her.

'Provided no emergency crops up prior to the party, of course you can go,' he assured her. 'And if it happened to be something really serious I probably wouldn't be able to make it either. But I certainly hope we'll both be at Tim and Vanessa's celebration.' He paused and when he continued speaking his voice had completely changed. 'After all, they've really got something to celebrate—five years of happy marriage!'

His tone had been low and bitter, and his eyes now held unmistakable pain. Taken aback at the suddenness of the change, Jan murmured her thanks and slipped past.

Would he be bringing his wife to the party?

She had no more personal conversation with him before Friday except for a brief moment when he returned her car keys with an assurance that all was now well with the engine, brushing aside her gratitude with an impatient shrug.

On Friday she kept her fingers crossed as the evening drew nearer, scarcely able to believe that nothing would prevent her going to the party. Making a quick round of Adam's patients as early as she dared, she finished with Mrs Felgate, who still occupied the side ward belonging to Nightingale.

Peter was there, paying a visit to his mother before going off duty, and he looked at her in surprise.

'What's this in aid of, Jan? Not that it isn't a pleasure to see you, but——'

'But you can't think why I'm here?' She laughed and explained.

'I'm very glad you're going to have a bit of fun, dear,' Margaret said in her gentle voice. 'While I've been here I've noticed how hard you work.' She turned to her son. 'I would have thought you'd be going with Jan, but you haven't mentioned it.'

'For a very good reason, Mum, I wasn't invited.' He smiled, but Jan detected an underlying resentment.

'I expect that's because it's all doctors,' Margaret suggested.

Jan did not disillusion her, though she would be very surprised if there were no nurses present, and she knew Peter must be aware of it too.

Most of the time he was content to be a charge nurse and proud to be responsible for two important wards, but every now and then he was reminded of how much he had wanted to be a doctor, and the sleeping chip on his shoulder stirred and gave him a painful prod.

For a moment she thought wistfully how much she would have liked to be going to the party with Peter as escort. He would have been a dear and familiar figure in a roomful of semi-strangers. It wasn't that she was shy, but it was always easier to arrive at a social occasion *with* someone rather than on one's own.

But when the time came and Jan reached the large downstairs flat in a quiet street behind the hospital, she found herself part of a small crowd who had all arrived at the same moment. The April evening was warm and windless, and the front door stood hospitably wide. It was easy to let herself be swept in among the others, and the first person she saw after greeting her hosts was Louise, glamorous in scarlet which went well with her dark curls.

'Cheers!' they toasted each other, and then each commented frankly on the other's appearance.

'I like that cream dress you're wearing,' said Louise. 'It's super with your colouring.'

'I get a bit tired of always having to consider my colouring,' Jan admitted. 'I'd love to be able to wear bright red like you, but I haven't the courage. When I was little my mother always used to make me wear green or blue, and I yearned for a nice red dress, or even a pink one.'

'Your mother isn't around now, is she?' Louise

asked carefully.

Jan shook her head. 'She died when I was fifteen, and I haven't any brothers or sisters.'

'God, you don't know how lucky you are! I'm one of six——' Louise broke off and looked over Jan's shoulder. 'Here comes your boss.'

'Has he got his wife with him?'

'Julie? You have to be joking! Why on earth should he be bringing her to a party? I should think he'd be glad to get out of reach of her demands for a while. The whole hospital knows what a nuisance she makes of herself. He must have the patience of a saint to put up with it.'

Jan smiled. 'I wouldn't have described him as a saint.'

'Nor me, but I only know him casually, of course. I told you I went out with him a few times, didn't I?'

Without waiting for an answer Louise turned to greet a good-looking male physiotherapist, and Jan drifted on to join a different group.

The party steadily became more crowded, and consequently noisier and hotter. Eventually Tim opened the french windows at the far end of the room and people poured into the garden for a breath of fresh air.

For nearly twenty minutes Jan had been pinned in a corner by Louise's boss, the balding and corpulent RSO. At first she had found him mildly interesting, but the need to supply a constant flow of brief but suitable replies to his semi-monologue was becoming something of a strain.

The general movement towards the garden gave her a chance to escape.

Finding her feet on a narrow brick path, she went wandering on towards the bottom of the long narrow garden where a large beech tree, perhaps once part of a much larger garden, offered a haven of momentary peace.

At first it seemed gloriously quiet under the spreading branches, and the noise of the party—not twenty metres away—had become no more than a blur of sound. But as her eyes grew accustomed to the darkness Jan realised she wasn't alone after all. Dimly seen couples were closely intertwined all around, and although they ignored her presence she felt a fool because she had joined them by herself.

If only Peter had been with her . . . they could have found a spot for themselves and also enjoyed a comfortable interlude. With a sigh Jan began to retrace her steps, but no sooner had she emerged from the shadow of the tree than she saw someone else coming down the path. Someone who was also alone.

'All by yourself, Jan? That's not allowed at a party.' Adam planted himself in front of her so that it was impossible to brush past him.

'Looks like you're breaking the rule too,' she suggested cheekily, and wondered why her heartbeats had quickened.

'That's easily remedied.' He tucked his arm in hers and turned her round. 'If we enjoy the night air together we're both safe from——' He paused and considered. 'What shall I say? In my own case it's colleagues who only want to talk about their own particular speciality and aren't interested in mine. In your case it's more likely to be over-amorous young doctors. Or am I wrong? Perhaps you enjoy their attentions.'

His tone had been light, but Jan gave the question her serious consideration.

'I don't enjoy being pawed by strangers,' she said decisively. 'I'm afraid I've never been very good at casual party pick-ups. But if I was with somebody I really liked—' her thoughts flew to Peter '—then I'd feel quite different about it.'

'Your attitude does you credit,' Adam said smoothly.

Was he laughing at her? Half ashamed because she must have sounded absurdly old-fashioned, Jan changed the subject.

'By the way, my father's boat went in the water yesterday.'

Adam was immediately interested. 'Did one of the local boatyards organise it for him?'

'Yes. He's got one of their moorings and he can get on board quite easily at high tide. He'd really rather be in a quieter position on the other side of the river, but he'd have to row across every time he wanted to go aboard, and that wouldn't be a good idea.'

'I don't suppose he can manage a rowing boat,' said Adam.

'Oh yes, he can! When he feels he must really get away from all the bustle he climbs into the dinghy and goes off on his own for a good hard row.'

'Good God!' On the verge of exclaiming at the risk taken by a man without the full use of his legs, Adam bit back the comment. No doubt Jan was already aware of the danger and wouldn't want to be reminded of it. 'You have to admire him,' he said instead. 'I shouldn't think there's much he can't do. Didn't he mention that he was still practising as a doctor?'

'Yes, but he only sees patients at the surgery. It helps him not to feel entirely useless, though.'

They had reached the shadow of the tree and its dark secret world swallowed them up. Jan's cream dress still showed up palely, but Adam's charcoal grey suit had melted into the background. Their faces were blurred and featureless, but there was nothing shadowy or insubstantial about the arm which held Jan's firmly. Her heartbeats, which had returned to normal during the slow stroll down the garden, now began to race at frightening speed.

'You're looking very attractive tonight,' Adam said softly, gathering up a handful of her hair and letting it slide sensuously through his fingers. 'You should always wear your hair loose.'

'No, I shouldn't,' she contradicted him breathlessly. 'I feel much more professional with it tied back.'

'Perhaps you're wise. Otherwise I might want to kiss you when we're on a ward round as much as I do now.'

'Oh!' Jan was still trying to keep them both on an even keel and she went rushing on. 'You told me off recently for letting my mind wander when I was working, but I'm quite sure you've got your own under strict control.'

'You'd be surprised!' he told her with a hint of laughter, and abandoned his fondling of her hair so that he could draw her more closely into the curve of his arm. Beneath his grey silk shirt his heart was thudding to equal hers, and the soft warm feel of her rounded body was stirring his senses in a way that was irresistible.

What the hell—there was no need for him to resist, and nothing in his experience had led him to believe she really wanted him to. And so he followed his instincts and bent his head to capture the lips which seemed freely offered. For a few moments they mutually savoured the sweetness of this unexpected interlude under the friendly beech tree.

Jan stood on tiptoe and slipped her arms round Adam's neck to draw his head even closer to her own. He could feel the fulness of her breasts pressed against him, and the sensation excited him still further. With an eager movement he slid his hand into the low neck of her dress.

It was a fatal gesture. Until then Jan had been swept along on a tide of emotion beyond her control. Now, suddenly, she was herself again, and she began to struggle.

'No, I don't want that—let me go, Adam—*please*!'

Neither of them noticed she had used his christian name. Adam was completely taken aback at the violence of her rejection. One moment she had been soft and yielding both mentally and physically, and now she was fighting him like an angry cat.

'What's the matter with you?' he demanded furiously.

'I told you I didn't like being pawed at parties.'

'You didn't mind at first—I swear it. And you said you didn't like necking with casual pick-ups. I'm not a stranger—I'm someone you see every day.'

Jan took a step backwards and faced him, whipping up her anger as she did so. 'There's another category of men I don't like being messed about by—*married* men! And you can't deny you're one of those.'

Turning on her heel, she fled back up the path to the safety of the crowd.

CHAPTER FIVE

FOR JAN the party was now definitely over. Luckily it was getting late and she could leave without causing comment. She hadn't brought her car, guessing it would be as quick to walk through a narrow lane leading to the hospital grounds, and she traversed it quickly, relishing the cool night air on her flushed face.

In her imagination she could still feel the hard pressure of Adam's mouth on hers, and the memory of her own tumultuous response was still strong. Reluctantly, she was forced to admit that her anger had been caused more by this than by his behaviour. He had, after all, only been following a fairly normal pattern.

So why had she minded so much?

It was a relief to plunge into the familiar hospital atmosphere, and a quick tour of her patients restored her still further. In Nightingale Mrs Felgate slept peacefully, but the night staff nurse was having trouble with a new patient who had been admitted to have a pace-maker fitted to her heart the next day.

'There's something worrying her, doctor,' the staff nurse said, 'but she won't tell me what it is.' Middle-aged herself, she looked dubiously at the girl with her mass of auburn curls and carelessly

pulled on white jacket not at all concealing the
party dress beneath. 'She may be more
forthcoming with you, but——' She left the
sentence unfinished.

Jan smiled to herself and went off to chat to
Miss Jameson, who turned out to be a retired
schoolmistress who had never been in hospital
before. With gentle perseverance she probed to
discover the cause of the patient's distress, and
was eventually successful.

'I absolutely dread having the mask put over
my face, doctor, and I'm so ashamed about it. I
mean, it seems so silly, but I've always been the
same. Couldn't bear trying on my gas mask in the
war——' She looked up piteously into Jan's face
as she bent over her in the dimly lit ward.

Jan was astonished at her ignorance and
hurried to reassure her. 'We don't do it like that
any more. You'll simply have an injection in your
wrist—just a quick prick—and you'll fall asleep
almost instantly. I'm told it's a very pleasant
sensation.'

'Oh, what a relief! I'm so grateful, doctor——'

'There's no need to be,' Jan smiled, and patted
her hand. 'I'm very glad I came along to set your
mind at rest. But just to make sure you have a
good night's sleep, I'll prescribe a pill for you.'

Leaving a much comforted patient, she said
goodnight to the staff nurse and toiled up to her
room, to lose herself within a few minutes in deep
refreshing sleep. By morning the memory of how
she had felt when Adam held her in his arms had

faded considerably.

Unfortunately she was reminded of it when she met him by chance after breakfast.

'By the way, Jan,' he hailed her abruptly, not bothering with a conventional greeting, 'it suddenly occurred to me this morning—when I was tying my tie, to be exact—that you might be labouring under a misapprehension, since you're new to the hospital. I'm not married now—I'm divorced. See you later.'

Jan gasped, her mind in a whirl, but uppermost in it was the realisation that he also must have been thinking about last evening.

It was all forgotten when they started operating. There was a long list of cases, among them Miss Jameson's pace-maker. As Jan watched Adam's nimble fingers fitting it, she marvelled at its ingenuity.

He must have sensed her absorption and his eyes smiled at her over the mask. 'Wonderful invention!' he remarked conversationally.

'I knew pace-makers existed, of course, but I've never seen one before.'

'You could learn to fit one yourself. Next time we have a case I'll teach you.'

Still talking, they followed the patient's trolley out of the theatre to have a quick break. 'This is my second job as a house surgeon,' Jan said, 'but I didn't find general surgery nearly as fascinating as your heart cases.'

'Specialising is always more interesting.' Adam ripped off his gloves and tossed them into the bin. 'If you're so keen on hearts why don't you stay with them? You could continue with me for an extra six months if you liked, and then get a junior registrar's job with a heart team somewhere. After that it would be up to you, but I wouldn't mind betting you could end up as a heart consultant yourself, in, say, ten years' time. There aren't many women in the field, but I don't see why there shouldn't be.'

Jan caught her breath as he outlined her possible future. It would be wonderful to do work she really loved and feel her feet firmly on the ladder at the same time.

But she mustn't even dream of it. She was destined for general practice and no way could she escape it. When her six months at Amberwell were up she would move on to a house physician's post elsewhere and concentrate on learning as much as she could about illness.

Fortunately the arrival of coffee spared her the necessity of replying, and she put the dizzy prospect Adam had outlined firmly out of her mind.

It was nearly lunchtime by the time they returned to the theatre, and Adam chose to work on without another break. Consequently, when they reached the end of their list, Jan was starving. As soon as she had taken off her operating gear she made a beeline for the canteen. To her surprise Peter was there, snatching a late tea break.

'What meal is that?' he asked, eyeing her plate

of two poached eggs on toast.

'Lunch!' she laughed, and began to eat hungrily. 'How's your mum today?'

'She's doing fine.' His blue-grey eyes glowed. 'I should think she'll soon be going to the convalescent home, won't she, Jan?'

'You'd better ask my boss that.' She smiled, pleased to see him looking happy again. 'I should certainly expect him to send her to the Anchorage rather than straight home because of there being nobody to look after her while you were working.'

Amberwell Hospital owned a convalescent home fifteen miles away at Shinglewick. It stood in a commanding position overlooking the sea and with gardens sloping gently down to the level of the promenade. Most patients were pleased to be sent there.

When the time came, a few days later, Mrs Felgate was no exception.

'It'll be just a lovely holiday,' she said contentedly as her son saw her into the ambulance. 'You'll come and see me as soon as you can, won't you, dear?'

'On my next day off,' he promised.

'See if Jan can come with you. It'll do her good just to sit and do nothing for a little while.'

Peter had already thought of the idea for himself, and when he made the suggestion he found Jan very willing to fall in with it if she could.

'I'd love to get a glimpse of the sea,' she said,

'and I've got a whole day free on Sunday. Would that fit in with your duty times?'

'I reckon I could make it fit,' he assured her confidently.

'Nice to be your own boss!' Jan laughed. 'I'd meant to spend the day with Dad,' she went on, 'and I shall have to visit him in the morning. But I could go to the Anchorage with you in the afternoon. OK?'

'Very much OK,' he agreed.

Jan always looked forward to her day off, but this week it attracted her more than usual. She was delighted to be awakened by the sun shining into her attic room and the day which had begun so well continued to be kind to her when she discovered her father had arranged to go sailing with his two friends that afternoon.

'I'd forgotten it was your day off, Janice,' Robert Latham admitted, 'but I'm sure you could come with us if you liked. How about it?'

She smiled. 'No, thanks, Dad. I won't intrude into your masculine atmosphere. I'm sure Jim and Ted are looking forward to getting away from femininity for a few hours! Besides, I've got something else lined up for this afternoon.'

'So you're going out with Peter,' he said thoughtfully when she had explained her intention. 'If you're not careful you'll end up marrying that young man.'

'Just because I'm spending Sunday afternoon with him——' Jan began indignantly.

'Don't be silly—it's not just that and you know

it. You've been close friends for years, and if you don't want to drift into marriage you'd better watch it.'

His interference aroused a contrary feeling in Jan. 'Why should I watch it? I'm very fond of Peter.'

'Boy and girl affairs which end in marriage are rarely a good idea. You know too much about each other. There's nothing left to discover and consequently no romance.'

With a swift change of mood, she laughed outright. 'What do you know about romance, Dad?'

'You'd be surprised,' he said darkly.

'I certainly would, and anyway, it's generally considered to be a good idea for doctors and nurses to marry each other. They've got so much in common.'

'You've shifted the basis of the argument. We're discussing lukewarm affairs that drag on, and not doctors marrying nurses. And I should think even that could be dicey when it's the woman who's the doctor and the man who's the nurse. Would Peter be content to run the home and answer the phone while you got on with doctoring?'

Finding herself cornered, Jan jumped up and announced her intention of seeing about the lunch. She prepared a light meal and saw her father off to join his friends at the river. He was as excited as a boy at the prospect of a sail, and she was delighted that he was to have that rather rare pleasure.

When she had washed up she drove back to the hospital to meet Peter. As she waited for him to join her in the car park, she debated whether she could suggest they used her car on such a lovely day. She already had the hood down, and the prospect of racing along the dual carriageway to the sea appealed to her immensely. Regretfully, she abandoned the idea. Peter would expect to drive his Fiesta and might even be hurt if she made it plain that she preferred her own.

He came striding out to join her just as she made her decision, looking attractive in a green shirt and swinging a light windcheater in his hand.

'Hi, Jan! Hurry up and get out of that heap of yours and into a proper car.' With a flourish he unlocked the Ford and held the door open for her.

Ignoring the insult to her precious vehicle because she didn't want to spoil the afternoon, Jan did as she was told. Peter drove through the town centre with care and precision, taking no chances at traffic lights, and soon they were on the road to Shinglewick. A lot of other people were going the same way on that beautiful Sunday afternoon and they did not talk much until a line of blue appeared in the distance.

'I'd love a swim,' Jan said wistfully.

'In the North Sea in May? You're out of your mind!' Peter carefully overtook a group of children wobbling along on bicycles.

'I suppose it would be rather cold. What time does visiting begin at the Anchorage?'

'Three o'clock. We're in nice time.' He turned along a road beside the promenade and then up a steep drive leading to the convalescent home. The gardens were gay with tulips and a huge bush of lilac filled the air with sweetness.

Margaret Felgate was sitting in an enclosed verandah, an unopened magazine on her lap and a look of dreamy content on her face. At the sight of her visitors she broke into a radiant smile.

'You've brought Jan with you! What a lovely surprise—how are you, my dear?'

'Fine! And having a super day off. How are you feeling?'

The reply was eminently satisfactory, and Jan sat down on a chair kept for visitors and allowed her thoughts to wander as mother and son talked. The blue sea still looked tempting and she wished she could run down the shingly beach and dip her fingers in the water, or pick up flat stones and play ducks and drakes like a schoolgirl.

The sun streaming through the glass was making her sleepy and she longed to fling the windows wide open. The patients wouldn't like that, though, and probably most of the visitors wouldn't either. Half listening to the conversation, mostly about domestic matters, she put in a word now and then but mostly remained silent.

Half an hour passed and she found herself wondering how long they would be expected to stay. Until four o'clock, she supposed, and took a surreptitious peep at her watch.

Was it possible she was actually finding it boring to spend the afternoon with these two old friends, of whom she was truly fond? Jan gave herself a mental shake and burst into the conversation with such animation that the others stared at her in surprise.

Later on, as they at last emerged into the fresh air, she said impulsively, 'Could we leave the car here for a little while and go for a walk?'

'A walk?' Peter was genuinely astonished. 'I should have thought both of us have spent enough time on our feet during the week without continuing on our free day. I could stagger as far as the nearest café, though.'

'Perhaps you'll be feeling a bit stronger after a cuppa?' Jan suggested.

He laughed and tucked his arm companionably into hers. 'Try me and see!'

They soon found a tea-shop and refreshed themselves with tea and toasted tea-cakes, after which they strolled along the promenade, dodging prams and tricycles and children with balls. The sun still shone and it was all very pleasant, yet still Jan felt out of tune with it.

'I wonder what Adam Delaney does with his time off,' she said suddenly, out of the blue, causing Peter to glance at her in surprise.

'Whatever made you think of him?'

'I don't know really. He—er—just popped into my head for no reason at all. You can't imagine him walking along the promenade at a place like Shinglewick, can you? I should think somewhere much more exotic would suit him better, like——'

'I don't particularly want to imagine him doing anything,' Peter interrupted. 'To me he's a darned fine heart surgeon and that's the end of it.'

'It can't really be the end of it.' Jan stepped aside to dodge an unsteady toddler, smiling down at the child as she did so and receiving a friendly beam in return. 'He must have other interests outside the hospital.'

'If he has he hasn't confided them to me.'

Peter was making no attempt to hide his increasing exasperation, but Jan seemed unaware of it. 'I should think he must have had quite a bit of social life when he was still married to Julie,' she said thoughtfully. 'Did you know her?'

'No, I didn't! I don't move in the same circles as consultants and their wives, you know.' They parted to allow a pram to pass between them and then he continued speaking. 'I knew Julie by sight, of course. I must say she was a good-looker—real blonde hair and a pair of enormous blue eyes. Just the sort blokes are supposed to fall for.'

'I didn't know they were divorced until recently,' said Jan. 'When Julie rang up about her car a little while ago and I answered the phone, she made such a fuss and was so demanding that I took it for granted they were still married and she had a right to expect Adam to sort it out for her.'

'From what I've heard she's the helpless type and perhaps he still feels an obligation to look after her, though if I remember rightly she was the one who went off with someone else and wanted a divorce.'

'Could be Mr Delaney's still in love with her,' Jan suggested, and had no idea how forlorn she had sounded.

'Maybe he is and maybe he isn't. Personally I couldn't care less. They could get remarried tomorrow and I wouldn't be the slightest bit interested.' Peter looked at his watch. 'Shall we turn round now and go back to the car?'

The wind had freshened and clouds were chasing each other across the sun, so Jan was very willing to do as he suggested. As they walked she began to talk about her father, wondering whether he had had a good sail. Peter was no more interested in sailing than in Adam Delaney's love life, but he seemed much more willing to discuss it. By the time they reached the car park they were once more on their normal friendly terms.

'Come back to the house and have some supper,' he urged as they neared the outskirts of Amberwell.

Jan turned a smiling face towards him. 'Does that mean you'd like me to cook you a meal?'

He laughed. 'You never used to be much good in the kitchen. Have you improved now?'

'I doubt it, but I'm willing to have a go with whatever you've got available.'

'Sounds too risky to me. I've become a passable cook while Mum's been in hospital, so I think I'd better make myself responsible for the meal and you can do the washing up afterwards.'

Jan made a face at him, but did not argue. In the end she helped with the vegetables and laid the table, and they both washed up after they had eaten the sausages, chips, and peas from the freezer provided by Peter.

'I suppose you've got to be back at ten?' asked Peter as they returned to the sitting-room.

'I start being on call then.' Jan sat down in an armchair, but immediately jumped up again. 'I wonder if there's anything worth watching on the box.'

'There's no need to keep leaping about.' Peter seated himself on the settee and patted the space beside him. 'We've got one of those remote control gadgets now. Mum said she'd like it and I never realised it was because she was feeling so tired. How blind can you get?' he added bitterly.

They found a programme which interested them and sat side by side watching it. Eventually Jan felt Peter's arm sliding round her shoulders and he drew her closer. Inevitably she relaxed and her head came to rest against his shoulder.

They had sat like that many times before and she felt quite at home, so much so that her eyelids began to droop. Permanently short of sleep as she was, it didn't take much to bring her to the verge of dropping off. After a while she did just that, her head heavy against him and her rebellious hair tickling his cheek.

A sudden change in the situation brought her abruptly back to consciousness. Peter's arm had tightened and his quiet, even breathing had quickened alarmingly. His lips were nuzzling her closed lids and, as she tried to open her eyes, they found her mouth.

Jan made a small sound of protest and moved her head. Startled at her reaction, Peter raised his own and stared down at her.

'What's up, love?'

'It's time to go—I don't want to be late——'

'There's at least another half-hour before you need even think of leaving. Plenty of time for——'

Her eyes dilated as she read his intention in his face and, inexplicably, she panicked. 'No, Peter. I'm sorry, but I'm not in the mood for romance.'

'Why on earth not?'

Jan began to struggle. 'I don't want to. Can't you accept that?'

'No, I can't.' He was still incredulous and, at the same time, hurt. 'You never used to mind.'

'That was *years* ago. We were teenagers then and all our crowd went in for necking—some of them in quite a big way. It's different now we're grown up.'

'I can't see that,' he grumbled.

Jan struggled to think of an explanation which would satisfy him. Perhaps she should tell him that the conviction which had kept her from 'going all the way' when she was younger—that lovemaking should be for real—still held good? It was certainly true.

But it wasn't the whole reason for her refusal. Luckily Peter did not press her for an explanation, and even seemed relieved when she said it was really time to go. They drove back to the hospital in silence, but Jan sensed that he had calmed down and perhaps forgiven her.

As they turned into the grounds, Adam's silver-grey Mercedes passed them on its way out.

'That was the boss.' Jan turned her head sharply. 'I wonder what he's doing here on a Sunday evening?'

'I hope it doesn't mean work for you.'

Jan hoped so too. When she got inside she went straight to the board where messages were left. But there was nothing for her, no urgent demand that she report to any of the wards, and she went thankfully upstairs to her room.

It was early to go to bed, but neither did she feel like going along to the doctors' common-room to see who was there, and eventually she settled down in her shabby armchair with a book.

Her precious day off, to which she had so much looked forward, had been something of a disappointment, though she couldn't quite understand why.

Or was it perhaps that she was *afraid* to understand?

CHAPTER SIX

ADAM had not had a satisfactory Sunday either, though it had started well with an energetic game of squash played against one of his regular opponents. He would have liked them to eat together afterwards, but his friend had a lunch engagement. Consequently Adam returned alone to his flat for a snack meal.

He was halfway through when the phone rang.

'I've been trying to get you all morning!' With a sinking heart he recognised Julie's high-pitched voice. 'Oh, Adam, I'm so terribly worried——'

'Is it the car again?' he asked in resigned tones.

'No, it's not the car. I've been terribly careful since you told me I was choking it and I believe you were right—though I didn't think so at the time—because I haven't had any further trouble.' She paused for breath.

'So what's the matter now?'

'It's me. Oh, Adam, I've got this awful pain in my inside and I've dosed myself with all sorts of things, but it doesn't get any better, and—I'm frightened.'

'Whereabouts is the pain?' He was no longer resigned but fully alert. 'Is it in your chest or the abdomen?'

'In my tummy,' she said childishly.

'When did it start?'

'Well, actually I've had it once or twice lately, but it always went off again, and I didn't want to trouble you unnecessarily,' Julie added virtuously.

He sighed and thought of the many times when she had not scrupled to trouble him unnecessarily—about her car, and the washing machine which had inexplicably flooded the kitchen, and the vacuum cleaner which came adrift from its plug.

When her romance with a local businessman had come to an end and he had abruptly left the town, Adam had allowed her to take over their old home—a miniature Georgian house in the old part of Amberwell—and he had moved into the flat over his consulting-rooms. He hadn't felt happy about the arrangement and would have preferred a clean break with his ex-wife as far away as possible. But Julie had been tearful, if not exactly heartbroken, assuring him pathetically that she would try very hard not to be any bother, but she really did need to stay near her friends at this unhappy time in her life.

Adam could understand how she felt, could even feel sorry for her, but his worst forebodings about the unsatisfactory nature of the arrangement had proved to be well founded.

'Have you thought of consulting your own doctor?' he asked now, and had no difficulty in guessing what her answer would be.

'I didn't like to trouble him on a Sunday, and I knew *you* wouldn't mind taking a look at me. I honestly don't think I can bear to wait until Monday, Adam—I really am in such dreadful pain!'

With an effort he hardened his heart. 'It's probably only indigestion.'

'Oh, Adam, how can you be so cruel!' There were tears in her voice.

He thought of her alone in the pretty little house, frightened and in 'dreadful' pain, and knew that, even if she was exaggerating—and she probably was—he was unable to resist her appeal. He had, after all, once fancied himself in love with her.

'All right,' he said curtly. 'I'll come along when I've finished my lunch.'

'Lunch? *I* haven't been able to eat a thing!'

'I've been playing squash and I'm hungry.' Adam looked at his watch. 'I'll be with you in about half an hour, but I hope you realise that what you're asking me to do is extremely unorthodox. I'm a heart specialist, not a general practitioner.'

As he had expected, the protest meant nothing to Julie. She'd never had any patience with medical etiquette.

'Oh, thank you, Adam darling,' she gushed. 'I knew you wouldn't let me down. I'll go back to bed now and try to wait patiently.' A sudden thought struck her. 'Have you still got a key?'

'As a matter of fact, I think I have, so you won't have to get out of bed to let me in.'

Replacing the receiver with unnecessary force, Adam cursed himself for his soft-heartedness, and at the same time admitted that no other decision had been possible for him. You never knew with abdominal pain. It might be severe indigestion, but it could also be an inflamed appendix or even a blockage.

He had avoided the little house ever since handing it over to his ex-wife; yet it did not seem strange to select the key from his ring and open the door. As he stepped into the familiar black-and-white tiled hall he heard Julie calling.

'Is that you, Adam?'

'Who else?' Determinedly closing his mind to ghosts from the past, he went steadily upstairs.

She was in the room they had shared, but all he could see of her in the double bed was a white face and two large blue eyes with a tangle of blonde hair on the pillow. A small part of his brain noted a trace of dark at the roots, and he hoped she wasn't letting herself go.

As he approached the bed he was for a moment overwhelmed by memories. Their shared happiness had been so brief, he could scarcely believe it had ever existed; much clearer now was the slow build-up of bitterness and regret, the inescapable knowledge that they had both made a terrible mistake.

'Oh, Adam, I'm so glad you've come!' Julie was saying weakly.

Whatever the origin of her pain, it seemed real enough. She winced as he palpated her abdomen, but he was unable to find that it had localised, though he gave her a long and careful examination and asked a great number of questions.

'Have you found out what's wrong with me?' she asked anxiously when he straightened up and pulled the duvet into place.

'I'm afraid not. So far it seems to be a mystery. I

suggest you try to put up with it for, say, another twenty-four hours and——'

'I couldn't possibly do that, Adam! I'd go mad lying here all alone and suffering so dreadfully and thinking all the time I might have got——' Julie shuddered and left the sentence unfinished.

Why did people always think of cancer when they had a bad pain? There were so many other things to choose from which weren't nearly so alarming.

'Isn't there anyone who could come and spend the night here?' he asked. 'One of your friends?'

'Nobody I'd care to ask on a Sunday.' Julie stretched out a slender arm clad in filmy pink silk and clutched his sleeve. 'Couldn't *you* stay, Adam? I'd feel safe then.'

'Good God—no, of course not!' He was outraged at the suggestion.

'There's no need to be like that! You used to *live* here, not so very long ago.'

'A great deal has happened since then,' he reminded her grimly. 'For one thing, we got divorced.'

'Sometimes I wish we hadn't,' she said softly, her huge eyes fixed on his face. 'Do you ever feel like that, Adam?'

In spite of the fact that he distrusted her sincerity, it seemed brutal to answer, 'No, I don't,' but it had to be said. He tried to soften it by adding, 'I think you're quite right not to want to be here on your own, so we'll just have to think of a solution.'

Julie had enough sense to keep quiet while he debated in his own mind what to do with her.

Eventually he came to a decision which was as unorthodox as his visit.

'I think you'd better be admitted into the private wing at the hospital for tonight, and then if you're still in pain tomorrow morning, various tests can be done to try and find out the cause.' Seeing her eyes widen with apprehension, he added persuasively, 'You'll be very comfortable there and the nurses will keep an eye on you. Would you agree to that?'

'Well, yes, I suppose so,' she said reluctantly, 'but I've never been in hospital and I can't help feeling a bit frightened.'

'There's no need, I assure you.' Adam turned towards the door with relief. 'I'll go down and get busy on the phone. I must make sure there's a vacant room and then square it with Manning, the RSO. Luckily I know him pretty well and he's a decent bloke. Then there's your doctor to put in the picture. God knows what he'll say.'

'Oh—er—I didn't tell you, but he's away on holiday, so you needn't bother to do anything about him. You'd only get put on to someone who doesn't know me and couldn't care less.'

'I see.' Adam looked down at her with a slight sarcastic twist to his lips. She had definitely said she didn't want to bother her doctor on a Sunday, but he refrained from reminding her. Julie had never scrupled to employ a small lie when it suited her.

He met with no opposition on the telephone, though James Manning, the RSO, couldn't resist adding, 'Let me make sure I've got the patient's name right, Adam. I gather she's still Mrs Delaney, but I rather thought she'd married some other bloke after the divorce?'

'That was the idea, but it didn't work out. I don't know the details—and I don't want to,' Adam added savagely.

The RSO let this pass and merely pointed out that there was no need for Adam to get involved any further if that was what he wanted.

'It *is* what I want, and I hope to God Julie understands.'

Unfortunately, it was soon made clear that Julie had no intention of understanding anything of the sort. For one thing, she obviously expected Adam to drive her to the hospital, and it scarcely seemed possible to refuse flatly and insist on her taking a taxi. To do so would have been a piece of callousness of which he knew himself to be incapable. But he did get her to pack her own suitcase, which she accomplished in a dithering sort of way, interspersed with heavy sighs, which nearly drove him mad.

'You'll stay with me for a little while, won't you?' she begged as they entered the lift which would deposit them on the private patients' floor.

Adam's eyebrows shot up and he made no attempt to disguise his reaction. 'Certainly not! The nurses will be much better at getting you settled than I would.'

Her eyes filled with tears and he immediately felt a brute. To his horror he heard himself weakly adding, 'I might look in this evening to make sure you're all right.'

She was pathetically grateful, and when—several

hours later and much against his will—he turned up he found her full of complaints.

'They haven't done anything for me at all, Adam, and I've still got this dreadful pain. The nurse said she couldn't give me anything stronger than Paracetamol until a doctor authorised it. Can't *you* do anything?'

'It's not my job.' He glanced round the bare little room and wondered if she had expected him to bring her flowers. 'I wouldn't like it if another doctor prescribed for my heart patients, and I've no intention of trespassing on the RSO's preserves. I expect his houseman will be around eventually.'

'His houseman? Do you mean he won't come himself?'

'That's precisely what I mean.' Adam sat down in a chair by the window and wondered how soon he could decently leave.

He endured fifteen minutes of listening to Julie's monotonous conversation, which he considered pretty generous, and then stood up and announced firmly that he was leaving.

He drove home in the depths of gloom and, when he finally reached his bed, found sleep eluding him. Visiting his ex-wife in the house they had shared had awakened memories of the past which he hoped were forgotten. They had been married in London three years before he took up his appointment at Amberwell, and for a time they had been happy. Even after Adam realised that their minds were as far apart as the two ends of a straight line, the physical attraction had remained. But not for long.

To make love to one's wife on a purely physical basis, without tenderness, was to diminish the whole experience and reduce it to the level of a casual affair. Almost certainly, Adam now realised, they would both have reached the stage of wanting a divorce even if Julie hadn't precipitated matters by running off with her new love.

He slept at last, unaware that he had forgotten to set his alarm, and woke up late. It was a bad start to a day which, he felt uneasily, might turn out to be as unsatisfactory as the previous one had been.

Jan, surprisingly glad that her day off was over and happy to be starting a new week, was totally unaware of the boss's ill-humour. Unfortunately she was a few minutes late when the team met at the nurses' station for a ward round in Simpson and Nightingale.

It was not her fault. One of Adam's patients had—like Mr Norbury earlier—been spending a couple of weeks in the Rehabilitation Unit and was now ready to be discharged. He had been taking a little exercise along the downstairs corridor and had buttonholed Jan to announce his progress.

'That's great, Mr Blackman!' she beamed at him. 'You'll be glad to get back to your home.'

'I won't be going back to the old flat, doctor, because that was upstairs. They've moved me to the ground floor—shifted all my bits and pieces and everything. They couldn't have done more, and I'll say that to anyone that criticises the Council.'

'I'm so glad.' Jan took a quick peep at her watch and excused herself hastily.

Unfortunately Adam and Tim had both arrived a little early, so that her tiny margin of lateness appeared worse than it really was.

'Good *afternoon*, Dr Latham.' Adam, who had avoided being late by breakfasting on black coffee—and found it totally inadequate—greeted her icily.

Jan flushed, muttered, 'Good morning, sir,' and burst into an explanation.

She was interrupted impatiently. 'I'm aware of Mr Blackman's progress, thank you, doctor. At the moment I'm much more concerned with my other patients. Shall we proceed?'

The tone in which he had spoken caused Jan's cheeks to burn even more brightly. Conscious that Tim had given her a cautious wink, and Peter was politely standing back to allow her to take her place in the procession, she swept past him with her head in the air. She could feel sympathy emanating from him and she didn't want him to be sorry for her. She could take care of herself, and even Adam in one of his black moods didn't scare her as much as he had done when she first came to work under him.

During the tour of Peter's two wards, Adam was grim, but managed to keep his temper under control. But as they went up in the lift to the private ward, Jan and the registrar were both conscious of a strangely increased tension in the atmosphere.

There seemed no reason for it. Adam had two patients up there—Mrs Green, the widow of a local headmaster, and Captain Steadman, a retired Naval man. Neither was giving any cause for concern and required only a brief courtesy call.

Escorted by the newly appointed and youthful Sister Barnes, back after a free weekend, the team trooped down the corridor preparatory to departure.

'Just carry on with the tablets in both cases, Sister,' Adam instructed, 'and in another day or so I'll think about reducing the dose.'

'Yes, Mr Delaney.' She looked at him innocently. 'Are you intending to visit your wife before you go? She was asking if you'd be round this morning.'

The silence which followed her question was probably no longer than a few seconds, but it seemed to Jan to go on for a very long time indeed. She glanced at Tim and saw that he was as surprised as herself. A strange sort of stillness seemed to hold the whole group immobile and incapable of speech. By the time Adam replied even Sister was beginning to look anxious, though she clearly had no idea what was wrong.

'Mrs Delaney,' said Adam ponderously at last, 'is not one of my patients.'

'Well, no, Mr Delaney—it's just that——'

'Furthermore,' Adam swept on, giving her no opportunity to finish, 'the patient to whom you are referring is no longer my wife. We were divorced some time ago.'

'Oh!' She went pink with embarrassment. 'I'm so sorry—I wasn't here when she was admitted and——'

'I know you weren't here, Sister.' Adam's grim face was momentarily illuminated by a charming smile. 'I'm not blaming you for the error—just putting you in the picture, that's all.' Turning on his heel, he stalked out of the ward and hurried down the stairs ahead of them.

'Well! What d'you know!' murmured Tim above Jan's head.

'I don't know anything,' she said. 'I wonder what Mrs Delaney's been admitted for?'

'I expect we shall soon hear. The grapevine'll get busy the moment the news breaks.'

Jan did not have to wait long to be informed of the situation. Wandering out into the grounds for some fresh air after a quick lunch, she found Louise sitting on a garden seat with her feet up and her eyes closed. Sensing she was being observed, she opened them quickly and made room for Jan to sit down.

'I was called out twice in the night,' Louise apologised, 'and the sun's making me terribly sleepy.' She yawned and rubbed her eyes.

'I'll go away if you like,' offered Jan.

'No, don't do that. I've only got five minutes and this seat is too uncomfortable for a nap anyway.' Another yawn overtook her, and when she had indulged it she sat up straighter and made an effort to pull herself together. 'I wouldn't have minded if both calls had been necessary, but one definitely wasn't. I suppose you know your boss's ex is in the private ward?'

'Sister referred to it on the ward round. She didn't seem to know there'd been a divorce.'

'Really? That must have been rather amusing. I can just imagine his reaction!' Louise suddenly became quite animated. 'The funny thing is, it was Delaney who admitted her. Don't you find that rather rum?'

The news was strangely unwelcome, but Jan did her best to hide the fact from Louise's sharp eyes. 'I find it rather rum that she's still Mrs Delaney,' she said in an offhand way. 'Peter told me she went off with another man and that was why they got divorced.'

'I daresay it was, but these grand romances don't always lead to marriage, love. Maybe Julie regrets what she threw away and would like to get Adam back. After all, he's very attractive if you can stand being bossed around, and he's got an assured position locally, with a long list of private patients and a super car. What more can a girl want?'

'To be loved, perhaps,' Jan suggested, and then, as Louise burst out laughing, wished she hadn't made such a corny comment.

'How do you know that wouldn't be available too if they came together again? She's a right so-and-so as a patient, but I should think she'd be good in bed. Maybe Adam would like to make it up? What do you bet?'

'Nothing,' Jan said curtly, 'but all the same, I wouldn't be a bit surprised if you're right.'

CHAPTER SEVEN

THE NEWS that Mr Delaney's ex-wife was in the
private ward was all over the hospital within a few
hours. The nurses found it intriguing and specu-
lated freely as to what the outcome might be. In
most cases the medical and surgical staff raised
eyebrows, shrugged and very quickly lost interest.
The exceptions were James Manning, the RSO, and
his team, who were treating the patient, and Adam's
own team, who were obliged to put up with his
black mood.

His temper was not improved by a conversation
he had with Manning when Julie had been nearly a
week in hospital.

'A word with you, Adam.' The RSO poured himself a cup of coffee from the filter jug in the
consultants' sitting-room, and sat down opposite the
heart specialist.

There was no one else in the room at the time and
Adam could think of no excuse for avoiding what he
guessed would be a discussion about Julie. He
merely said, 'Yes?' and glowered at the plump
middle-aged figure opposite.

'Did you know Mrs Delaney has given you as her
next of kin?'

'Good God!' Adam was aghast. 'Surely she could
think of someone else?'

94

'Apparently not. Her parents are in New Zealand, I believe, and as you're here on the spot——'

'On the spot just about describes it!' Adam sipped his coffee gloomily and brooded. 'I suppose there's something to be said for it,' he acknowledged, 'but I don't at all care for it and I hope you're not going to tell me I'm likely to get involved. There's nothing seriously wrong with her, is there?'

'We haven't been able to find anything except a possibility of gall bladder trouble. If the pain recurs it might be a good idea to explore more thoroughly.'

'Have you told her?'

'Not yet, but I intend to do so later today, and after that I shall discharge her.' James smoothed his thinning hair. 'I thought you'd like to know—er—in case you want to visit her before she leaves.'

'I don't *want* to, but I suppose I'd better. I have to confess I haven't been near her since she was admitted. I knew you'd keep me informed.'

With a violent movement which nearly overturned his chair Adam got up and strode over to the window, where he stood staring at the trees in a nearby park. Sensing that there was more to come, James waited quietly.

'I can't tell you how desperately I want to avoid being involved,' Adam went on savagely. 'Julie is the clinging type, who must have a man in her life. She had me once, and it wasn't an enjoyable experience after the first enthusiasm wore off. I have to admit it was a great relief she left me.'

It was unlike him to unburden himself so freely, but the RSO had learned not to be surprised by anything. He filled the pause with a judicious nod and continued to drink his coffee.

'I can't help wondering if she'd like to pick up the threads of our marriage and start again.' Adam turned round and glowered at the floor, his hands in his pockets. 'Sometimes, James, I feel that if I don't watch it I shall be trapped into agreeing.'

'That's ridiculous! If you let yourself get trapped you'll only have your own weakness to blame. I should have thought you were far too strong-minded to let anything like that happen.'

'I hope to God I am,' Adam said fervently.

James put down his cup and stood up. 'I'd better relinquish the role of Agony Aunt and go and break the news to Mrs Delaney that there's nothing much wrong with her. I shan't say too much about the possibility of gall bladder trouble—I don't want to scare her. As for you,' he added, his hand on the door knob, 'the best thing you can do is find yourself another wife. You're over thirty and it's time you settled down.'

Adam shrugged the advice aside. He'd had enough of marriage and had no wish to endanger his liberty a second time. Not yet, anyway.

He put off visiting Julie until the evening, and when he reached the private ward he was surprised to find her room empty.

Had she left already? His sense of relief was quickly stifled by the sight of her toilet articles on the dressing-table and a scatter of magazines on the bed.

Questioning a nurse whom he met in the corridor,

he was informed that Mrs Delaney was in Room 14, visiting Captain Steadman. Seeing Adam's astonishment, the nurse added hastily, 'Mrs Delaney hadn't got a book to read tonight and Sister thought the Captain might lend her one of his libraries. He's always got a great pile.'

It seemed a valid reason for visiting a stranger, though Adam doubted if Captain Steadman's taste in books was the same as Julie's. As he hesitated whether to visit both of them, or make his escape, the nurse intervened.

'I'll go and tell Mrs Delaney you're here, sir.'

Room 14 was only two doors away and Adam plainly heard Julie's reply. 'Adam here? Then why doesn't he just come along? Captain Steadman is one of his patients.'

There was nothing for it but to do as she suggested, and Adam found himself making an unwilling third at what seemed to be a remarkably jolly social occasion.

The Naval man, wearing an old-fashioned but elegant maroon silk dressing-gown, was sitting in an armchair by the window. He had thick grey hair, good features and a firm mouth. Julie, clad in a pretty blue velvet kaftan trimmed with lace, was perched on the bed and appeared to be enjoying herself. Looking at her, Adam could scarcely believe she had recently suffered such severe pain.

'There's no need to ask if you're feeling better!' he exclaimed when he had greeted his patient.

'Well, the pain hasn't *quite* gone, but I don't think about it when I'm interested in something. Captain

Steadman and I have been having a lovely long talk about his days at sea. Do you know, Adam, he actually met my uncle David who was in the Navy too. They were both based at Gosport. Isn't that an amazing coincidence?'

Adam didn't think it particularly surprising, since people in the Services were always meeting each other, but he agreed with her politely and allowed her to chatter on.

After a few minutes it became obvious that the Captain was finding the situation embarrassing. When Adam came in he had been smiling and cheerful, clearly enjoying the company of his attractive visitor; now he had relapsed into an uncomfortable silence. It was time to go.

'I hear you're being discharged tomorrow,' Adam said to Julie.

'Yes, Mr Manning told me today.' She flashed him a slightly malicious smile. 'My taxi has been ordered.'

So she wasn't expecting him to drive her. Relieved and also somewhat surprised, Adam merely said a vague, 'That's good.' At the door he felt something more was called for and added, 'I hope you won't have any more pain, but if you do please contact your doctor at once.'

'Mr Manning said that too, so I suppose I'd better do as I'm told.'

'Certainly you had. Er—good luck.'

Outside the door he breathed a sigh of relief and hoped fervently that Julie would now settle down to making a new life for herself. She was very attractive in a slightly outdated way and had plenty of casual friends. There was no need for her to mope alone—or plague her ex-husband with constant appeals for help.

Unless he was right in the suspicion he had mentioned to the RSO—that she wanted to rekindle the dead ashes of their marriage.

Shying away from the thought with the utmost horror, Adam gave himself a hearty mental shake. A sudden longing to get away from the familiar atmosphere of the hospital seized hold of him, to breathe fresh invigorating air and battle with the elements.

He remembered the boat he had seen propped up in Jan's father's garden. *Sea Lady.* Hadn't Dr Latham offered him a sail in her when he could find the time?

It became of the utmost urgency that he should find Jan and question her on the prospects of taking a trip.

He waylaid her as she was starting her late round. Surprised to see him in the hospital at that hour, since she knew of no emergency, Jan said a polite, 'Good evening, Mr Delaney,' and waited to be told what he wanted of her. His first words were unexpected.

'How's your father, Jan? Is he getting some good sailing?'

'Not as much as he would like, but he's had a few trips.'

'I expect he finds it difficult to arrange—the tide and his crew's availability and all that.'

'You can say that again!' laughed Jan. 'He had a super sail last Sunday, but as far as I know he's got nothing else lined up.' Puzzled, she looked up into Adam's brooding face and suddenly remembered the invitation her father had extended. The boss looked much in need of a real break from hospital routine. His eyes were tired, as though he hadn't been sleeping, and there was a tautness round his mouth.

'Were *you* thinking of offering yourself as crew?' she asked impulsively.

Adam's whole face changed as he smiled. 'That's exactly what I had in mind. Do you think there's any prospect of fixing a sail?'

'Every prospect, I should think, provided you can fit it in yourself. Dad only works part-time, you know, so it isn't difficult for him. The thing is——' She hesitated, anxious not to banish the sudden cheerfulness before it had even got properly established.

'The thing is—what?'

'Well, my father can't do much himself and he likes to have *two* others with him. *Sea Lady*'s a fair-sized boat.'

'I see.' Adam relapsed into thoughtfulness. 'Couldn't you come, Jan?' he asked suddenly.

'Me? Oh, but——' She broke off in confusion, more disturbed by the suggestion than she cared to admit. 'I'm not very experienced,' she went on doubtfully. 'I don't know if my father would consider me adequate.'

'We can ask him.'

'Yes, of course, but—well, how would I find the

time? It wouldn't be worth while going if I hadn't got a whole afternoon and evening free.'

'You must have *some* time off, for goodness' sake.' Adam thought for a moment and then came to a rapid decision. 'Give me your father's phone number,' he ordered, 'and I'll sound him out. After that, if he's agreeable, you can safely leave it to me to fix it so you have enough time.'

A few days later Jan was surprised to be greeted by Tim with a strangely knowing smile and an interesting item of information.

'I hear you're going sailing with the boss tomorrow,' he remarked.

Not liking the smile, she said airily, 'It's the first I've heard of it.'

Tim raised his bushy eyebrows. 'You must have known something about it, surely?'

'Well, yes. I knew my father had invited Mr Delaney to join him for a sail, but that was ages ago. I expect they're only taking me along as another crew member.'

'Oh, I see.' Tim sounded disappointed.

Glad that she had managed to divert his mind from the direction it seemed prepared to take, Jan awaited Adam's instructions. They came at the end of the morning.

'We're starting at two o'clock, Jan.' Adam was as excited as a schoolboy. 'Your father says the tide will be just right then. Apparently the parking down by the river is limited, so we'd better take your little car instead of mine. Besides, I'd like to try it. I take it you'd have no objection if I drove?'

'Oh no, sir, none at all,' Jan said meekly.

She had overdone it a bit and was given a suspicious glance, but Adam made no comment and he did not refer to the outing again until they met in the car park the following day.

It was a perfect day for sailing. Small white clouds chased each other across a blue sky, driven by a stiff westerly breeze, and the sunshine ensured a reasonable degree of warmth. Both Jan and Adam were in jeans and T-shirts, and carried thick sweaters in case of need.

Jan had slipped out a short time earlier and started her car, just in case it should be unco-operative when the time came. Now, to her relief, the engine sprang into life at Adam's first attempt, and with the hood down, they swept down the drive and out into the road.

It seemed strange to be a passenger in her own car, and even more strange to be driven by the boss. Strange and yet rather nice too, since Adam was obviously so very competent. Relaxing in her seat, Jan found herself wishing the journey had been longer.

It took only ten minutes to reach the River Amber, which flowed along the southern edge of the town, surprisingly wide when the tide was high, and consisting mostly of mud with a narrow deep-water channel when it was low. Robert Latham was there before them and had already transferred himself to the boat, which was tied up to a jetty and had a wider than normal gangplank with firm handrails.

Knowing her father so well, Jan could see he was

a little dubious about his crew, but as Adam appeared to understand the instructions given him and she did her best to play her own part, they cast off without incident.

'The tide's still making,' said Robert, 'so we'll take advantage of it and go up-river first. See how we get on.'

'It's wide like this for about another mile, isn't it?' Adam asked when the mainsail was up and they were skimming over the water.

'That's right. It narrows very suddenly and the whole character changes.' Robert's hand tightened on the tiller. 'Watch it now—I'm going about.'

As she dodged the swinging boom and moved to the other side of the boat, Jan felt the wind snatch at the ribbon tying her hair. Before she could do anything, it had gone and the loosened hair streamed out behind her as though she were a figurehead on one of the old sailing ships. Drawing in great breaths of the pure sweet air, she realised that her perpetual tiredness had vanished, blown away by the wind. It was even better than driving her car with the hood down.

Adam had changed too. He was a totally different person from the haunted man who had suggested the outing. He looked five years younger and ten times happier. His dark hair was on end and the lines of strain had left his face, leaving only laughter lines and the creases made by screwing up his eyes against the sun.

As she moved across the boat yet again, Jan was very conscious of his powerful lean maleness so near her. She was used to seeing him correct in a well-cut suit, not clad in skin-tight jeans and a skimpy shirt which revealed muscular arms and thick dark hair on his chest. The transformation was oddly disturbing.

Perhaps it was because her mind wasn't entirely on what she was doing that they made a mess of the turn-about which Robert had decreed. The manoeuvre was certainly amateurish and Robert used bad language when a sail flapped frantically. Fortunately, because it was mid-week, the only spectators were the cows lazily staring from lush water meadows.

'Sorry, sir,' Adam apologised.

'You're doing very well on the whole.' Robert Latham had rapidly recovered his temper. 'A little more practice would make a quite reasonably competent sailor of you.'

Jan glanced at Adam from beneath her lashes and had no difficulty in discerning that the kindly meant remark had not pleased him. He wouldn't be content with being 'quite reasonably competent' at anything. For the first time she realised how the failure of his marriage must have irked him, apart from the distress he had presumably suffered.

'Stop daydreaming, Janice!' Her father's tone was caustic. 'If you want to make yourself useful, go and put the kettle on.'

Jan gave herself a mental shake and descended to the tiny galley. It was ridiculous to spoil such a perfect afternoon by thinking about an unpleasant subject like Adam's marriage, and she was glad to have been interrupted.

They passed Amberwell again, its numerous boatyards crowding the quayside and a forest of masts in the dinghy park, and went on down-river. With both tide and wind now in their favour, they made good progress and there was no need for continual watchfulness. Robert even allowed Adam to take the tiller and relaxed on a comfortable seat in the cockpit. As Jan stood beside him, holding on to the coaming and swaying with the movement of the boat, she knew that never before had she so much enjoyed an afternoon on the river.

It was due to the wonderful weather, of course. In her experience it was rare to have no need to huddle in oilskins and grapple with wet sails, or cling on perilously as the boat fought against wind and water at an angle too acute for comfort.

It was eight o'clock when they returned to the jetty and tied up again. Stowing the sails under Robert's eagle eye and generally making all tidy took some little time, since Adam was anxious to acquit himself well. Jan helped as best she could, trying to follow her father's barked out orders and not make a fool of herself.

As she worked she was conscious that her mood of happiness and content had vanished, to be replaced by something very close to depression. She told herself it was because she was tired and hungry. Her blood sugar was probably low, which was well known to have a mental effect as well as a physical one.

Anxious that her change of mood shouldn't be

noticed, she thanked her father with tremendous enthusiasm for an 'absolutely fantastic sail.'

'Glad you enjoyed yourself.' He gave her a pleased and yet slightly puzzled look. 'I used to think you weren't all that keen on sailing.'

'Nobody could have helped enjoying it on such a super afternoon,' she said evasively.

Not even to herself was she willing to admit that it hadn't been only the weather which had made her so happy.

'You two push off now,' ordered Robert. 'I'm perfectly capable of getting myself back to my car unaided, and I don't want an audience while I'm doing it.'

'I was wondering if you'd care to have a meal out somewhere,' Adam suggested.

'No, thanks. My housekeeper has left me something ready and she won't appreciate it tomorrow if I haven't eaten it.' Evidently feeling he had not been very gracious, Robert added hurriedly, 'Kind of you to offer.'

There had never been any hope that he would accept, Jan knew that, and yet her heart had leapt in the most absurd fashion. Once more she put it down to acute starvation.

Adam was looking at her with strange intentness, almost as though he hadn't seen her before. On the boat, of course, she had merely been the other half of the crew; now he must have suddenly realised how appallingly untidy she looked.

In actual fact she was looking very attractive with her mass of chestnut hair glowing above the creamy

wool of her sweater, and her skin just sufficiently
burnt by wind and sun to give her a healthy colour.
Even the scattering of freckles on her nose fitted in
with the general picture.

'How about you, Jan?' asked Adam.

'I'd adore a meal out!' She made no attempt at
pretence, but hastily explained her enthusiasm by
adding, 'I was just thinking of the unexciting food I
was going to get in the canteen. Not that I'm not
hungry enough to eat anything——'

'That makes two of us, so let's be on our way.'
Adam plunged into his navy blue guernsey and
pulled it down over his jeans. 'I'm afraid it will have
to be a pub meal. We're not dressed for anything
else.'

'I like pub food. Thick slices of home-made brown
bread and great chunks of cheese, or perhaps a
curry——'

'I'll settle for the curry,' Adam laughed, and
tucked his arm in hers.

When they reached the little car, he got into the
driver's seat without asking permission. Not that Jan
minded. Somehow it seemed perfectly natural.

CHAPTER EIGHT

ADAM chose a pub by the river in a small village about five miles away. Thatched roof, hanging baskets filled with red geraniums, oak beams and a log fire, all made it a popular venue for Amberwell people. The bar was crowded, but the restaurant built out at the back had room to spare.

The curry they both had hoped for was on the menu and they were soon enjoying great heaped platefuls of it, washed down with ice-cold lager. At first they were too hungry to talk but, later, as they drank cup after cup of coffee, the power of speech returned at full strength.

'I don't know when I've seen you looking so healthy,' Adam commented, staring at Jan across the table.

'Meaning that I'm normally what my Scottish grandmother used to call "peelie-wallie"?' Her hot cheeks burned even brighter.

'If that means pale and tired-looking, then it's exactly what I do mean.'

'Thanks very much!'

He was unimpressed by her pretended indignation. 'All housemen—and housewomen—look like that.' Holding out his cup for a refill, he continued, 'Do you think your father would put me on his list of possible crew? I'd appreciate it very much.'

'I should think he'd be glad to. His two chief mates are both married and can't always get away.'

Lost in thought, Adam sipped his coffee. 'There's just one problem,' he said eventually. 'He might not be prepared to put up with me on my own and I don't know who would make the third member. Obviously it wouldn't always be possible to fix it so you could come.' Across the table his dark sea-blue eyes held hers. 'Much as I should like it.'

He was only being polite, of course, though she had to admit that politeness wasn't his usual line. Brutal frankness would be nearer the mark!

'You'll just have to wait and see,' she said vaguely, and was not surprised to see the remark hadn't pleased him.

They were silent for a moment and then Adam said, 'Did you tell me your father sometimes goes off in the dinghy by himself?'

'Yes, he does.'

'I don't see how it's possible.'

'It certainly is, but as I've never seen him set off—thank goodness!—I don't know how he manages. He'd be OK once he was afloat because his arms are tremendously strong. He can probably row a lot better than either you or I could.'

'Better than you anyway,' he amended with a smile.

Inevitably, after a while, they began to talk shop. Jan was surprised to find Adam had remembered the suggestion he had made to her some time ago that she should aim for a career in cardiology.

'Of course you're a bit young for specialising,' he said, 'but if you've made up your mind where your interests lie—and yours obviously lie in hearts—then you should begin to plan the future.'

Jan's relaxed contented mood melted away like morning mist. She didn't have to plan the future—it was already done for her.

'But I can't possibly—I'm not free to choose!' she exclaimed in such an anguished voice that Adam stared at her in astonishment.

'Not free? Why on earth not?'

'I have to go into general practice.'

He frowned, drawing his thick black brows into a straight line. 'For heaven's sake! Nobody can make you become a GP if you don't want to!'

'I couldn't bear to disappoint my father,' she said simply.

Light dawned on Adam. Whether consciously or not, Dr Latham had been exercising strong moral pressure, and Jan was too fond of him to resist. He boiled with indignation and then, on the verge of bursting into a condemnation of parents who tried to order the lives of their offspring, got a grip on himself. The poor chap had a lot to put up with in his severely crippled state and his own career blasted years before its end. It was natural he should want Jan to carry on in his place.

Natural—yes. But certainly not right.

'I can see why you don't want to disappoint him,' he said thoughtfully, 'but I think you should at least try to put up a fight. Couldn't you instil into his mind gradually that you have other ideas? Let him down gently?'

'No.' Jan's full red lips set in a firm line. 'I haven't told you the whole story yet, Adam. It's a family practice, you see, and I'd be the third Dr Latham in it. My grandfather was the first.'

He looked at her in bewilderment. 'I can't see that that makes any difference.'

'But of course it does, Adam. Haven't *you* got any family feeling?'

He shook his head. 'I never had any family.'

'Never? You mean——'

'I was an only child, like yourself, the difference being that my parents divorced when I was very young. They tossed me about between them until I was old enough to take charge of myself. That sort of upbringing doesn't give you a sense of family.'

Impulsively Jan stretched across the table and put her hand on his, her wide hazel-green eyes soft with sympathy. 'What an absolutely horrible start to life! No wonder you can't understand why I want to please my father.' She paused, but he said nothing and allowed his hand to remain where it was. Emboldened, she went on softly, 'I'd just like you to know that working with you, watching you operate and being allowed to help has been the most thrilling experience of my whole life.'

As soon as the words were said, she was appalled at herself. How could she have given voice to anything so maudlin? Adam would be utterly disgusted. Fearfully, she stole a glance at his face, expecting at the very least to see him looking amused.

Far from it. It almost seemed that her impulsive tribute had touched him. He gave her hand a quick squeeze and said quietly, 'Thanks, Jan. That's the nicest thing anybody ever said to me.'

They did not stay long after that, for Jan had to be back by ten o'clock. As they left the little riverside inn she glanced up at the pretty frontage now decked with coloured lights. It had been a perfect setting for the last act in an afternoon and evening made up of much varied happiness.

But it wasn't the last act. Not by any means.

'I think we ought to put the hood up,' Adam decreed, beginning work on his side. 'It's turning cold.'

Jan had shivered as she came out of the warm pub and she made no protest. Besides, she wouldn't want to leave the car unprotected at the hospital.

Adam removed his heavy sweater and got in. Snug and intimate in the tiny interior, they set off on the short drive to Amberwell. Jan leaned back comfortably, tired after her exertions on the boat and sleepy after large quantities of fresh air followed by good food and drink. A delicious inertia took possession of her and she wondered why Adam was driving so fast.

After a while he said, 'Pity we sat so long over supper. We shan't have much time for saying goodnight.'

Jan jerked wide awake. 'We're not late, are we?'

There was a tiny pause before he answered. 'Not

really. I just thought it might be pleasant to turn off this busy road and find somewhere quieter—for saying goodnight.'

Her heart thudding in her ears, she wondered if she had heard aright. But there was no mistake. Within a few minutes Adam had swung the car into a tree-lined lane and reduced his speed to a crawl. As Jan sat tautly in her corner he found what he was looking for—a field entrance.

The car bumped off the road on to a grassy verge. As he switched off the engine a tremendous silence caught them in its grip, or so it seemed at first. Then the small noises of the night began to make themselves heard, the sleepy twitter of a late bird, the rustle of some small animal in the undergrowth and—more distant—the barking of a dog.

Loudest of all, it seemed to Jan, was the beating of her own heart.

Adam said complacently, 'This will do very nicely. Much better than the hospital car park.'

He turned in his seat and reached out for her blindly, urgently, his lips eager to taste the sweetness of hers and his hands groping for the soft warm flesh beneath the big sweater.

'You're all encased in wool—I can't find you inside that huge garment.' He began to tug at it, lifting it up and over her head.

She offered no resistance even when her T-shirt came off along with the sweater. With a small wriggle of sensual delight she nestled up against him and felt his fingers struggling with the fastening on her bra. As he succeeded in undoing the hooks and she felt his eager hands caressing her bare back, a glorious tingling sensation crept over her whole body. She closed her eyes and waited for him to recapture her mouth.

But suddenly there were lights coming along the lane and the rough sound of a powerful engine. Something huge and dark lumbered into view and stopped a few yards away.

'Sorry, mate!' A disembodied voice reached them, its owner high above them in the tractor. 'Afraid I'll have to disturb you—I want to get through that gate.'

'Hell!' Adam thrust Jan from him with a violent movement and restarted the engine as she cowered in her seat, trying to hide her nakedness.

The car backed off the grass with a jerk that flung her against the door, but somehow she got her bra done up again even though her fingers were clumsy with panic. Half in and half out of her shirt, she was whirled back towards the main road.

'What the devil is a bloody great tractor doing out at this time of night?' Adam demanded when they had resumed their journey towards Amberwell.

'I think they sometimes work in the fields after dark when the weather's suitable,' Jan offered in as normal a tone as she could manage.

There was a silence and then he said thoughtfully, 'Perhaps it was just as well that bloke came along just then. If he hadn't I might have let myself get carried away.'

There was no answer to be made to that and Jan

attempted none. She had come crashing down from a peak of crazy happiness and was feeling utterly shattered by the experience. It would take her every minute of the time she had left to repair the façade she presented to the hospital world, so she could face Tim with equanimity when she went on duty. But it wasn't that easy and she feared there might be cracks which only time could mend. If anything did.

They reached the hospital and drove to the quiet corner of the car park which Jan made her own. As she got out she glanced uncertainly across at Adam, who was locking the driver's door. In the harsh light of an overhead lamp he looked brisk and businesslike, and she guessed that the return to the familiar scene meant he was once more Adam Delaney, FRCS, head of the Cardiac Department, and she the most junior member of his team.

'I'll come with you,' he said casually, 'in case Tim has anything of interest to report.'

It wasn't flattering to find he had resumed his normal role with so much apparent ease, whereas with herself it was completely different. As they walked towards the side door she could still in imagination feel the pressure of his mouth on hers, and the soreness of her burning skin would remind her for some time that her boss was a man who needed to shave twice a day.

They found Tim in the doctors' sitting-room and he greeted them with a cheerful smile.

'You two look on top of the world!' he exclaimed.

Jan's colour deepened still further, but Adam said calmly, 'We had a wonderful sail. It's made me feel I really must do something about getting a boat of my own.' He sat down on the arm of a chair. 'Anything happened?'

Tim's smile faded. 'Caroline's back again. I admitted her a couple of hours ago.'

'That's bad, but not unexpected.' Adam sighed. 'The intervals at home are definitely getting shorter. Is she comfortable now?'

'That well-worn hospital phrase fits very well in her case. She's as well as can be expected.'

'I'd like to see her before I go, but I don't want to disturb her if she's asleep.' Adam stood up decisively. 'I'll go along to Nightingale and assess the situation. You'd better come with me, Jan.'

They walked in silence through the quiet corridors and came to Nightingale Ward. Caroline was in the side ward which had been occupied by Mrs Felgate and, although obviously sleepy, seemed delighted to see Adam.

'Mr Delaney!' A thin hand came out and clasped Adam's affectionately. 'How lovely of you to come and see me!' The large blue eyes gazed up into his face with obvious adoration.

'As soon as I heard my favourite patient was here, of course I came along.' He smiled down at her, his expression softer than Jan had ever seen it. 'Now that I'm here, is there anything I can do for you?'

She shook her head languidly, not lifting it from the pillow where her beautiful corn-coloured hair had been spread out by a nurse. 'No, thanks. I'm fine now and the pain has quite gone.' Her voice was weak and breathless. 'I feel wonderfully sleepy now and I think I'm going to have a good night.'

'You've got your bell handy?' He located it pinned to the pillow. 'Don't hesitate to summon Nurse if you need her, and Dr Latham here will come and see you if it's necessary. Not that I think it will be.'

Jan hoped fervently she would not be called from her bed to attend this very ill patient who was obviously dear to Adam's heart. She had never been left in charge of such a serious heart case before and she knew it would be hard to have faith in her own judgement.

Adam too seemed to have doubts about her. He was emphatic she was not to waste time dithering if she needed help but to get straight on to the phone and summon him to the hospital.

'Even if you're afraid I shall tear you off a strip for getting me out of bed for nothing. I probably shall, but having to put up with that—' a grim smile twisted his lips '—is better than running a risk with a girl as ill as Caroline.'

'Wouldn't it be wonderful if she could have a transplant?' Jan said wistfully. 'Is there any hope at all?' Seeing his expression, she apologised, 'I'm sorry—that was a silly question which you can't possibly answer.'

'We've done all we can do. I sent her to Harefield and got her assessed and they seemed to think a transplant would be quite possible. Unfortunately, life for Caroline means death for someone else, but as I know Caroline and the donor would presumably be a stranger, I'm hoping I shall be able to concentrate on the transplant and ignore the tragedy behind it. That is, of course, if a suitable heart turns up before it's too late.'

For a few moments Adam had spoken to her as though to a medical equal, and Jan couldn't help a small tremor of appreciation in spite of the gravity of his words. She said a rather breathless goodnight and set off on a quick tour of the hospital as though she were being wafted along on a cushion of air.

She found nothing about which she needed to worry. Tim had already dealt with various small problems concerning drug dosage and other matters, and soon she was free to retire to her attic room and hope the phone wouldn't ring. Or, if it did, it wouldn't be because Caroline was worse.

Because she was tired and had had a lot of fresh air, she fell asleep quickly. When the alarm woke her hours later, she could scarcely believe she had been lucky enough to have a completely undisturbed night.

Before she went to the canteen for breakfast, she hurried to see how Caroline was and found she had also had a good night. Peter was in his office and seemed surprised to see her so early.

'You're looking very blooming!' he exclaimed.

'I'm feeling blooming too,' Jan said lightly. Seeing his eyebrows lift slightly, she added an explanation. 'I had a marvellous sail yesterday with—with my father.'

He looked down at her thoughtfully, his expression sombre. 'Just you and the old man?'

'No, of course not. There had to be a third

person to make it safe—I'm not very experienced.' As Peter continued to study her with that strange expression, she added defiantly, 'Mr Delaney came with us. Dad had promised him a sail when he could fix it.'

'So that's how he came to be driving your car!'

Her temper was bubbling, but she tried to control it. 'What on earth do you know about that?'

'He was seen approaching the hospital in it last night.'

'So what? I was there too.' Jan tilted her chin angrily. 'Who saw us, anyway?'

'One of my nurses returning after her day off.' Peter hesitated and then continued, 'And that's not all. I didn't mention it at the time, Jan, but you were seen a while ago coming down the attic stairs with your boss.' Seeing her about to explode, he went on hastily, '*I* don't for a moment imagine there isn't a perfectly innocent explanation, but I don't think it's wise to lay yourself open to gossip. You know what the grapevine's like in a hospital.'

Jan took a deep breath and got a grip on herself. 'I wish people would mind their own business! Why on earth should anyone think it necessary to report back to you on my movements? In my opinion it's downright bloody cheek!'

Peter shrugged. 'I suppose it's because they know we're—friends.'

'Very likely.' She hesitated, trying to choose between an inner compulsion which was urging her to tell Peter the true story of Adam and herself in the attics, and a strong reluctance to do so. Eventually she found herself explaining casually about going up to fetch her car keys and being followed because Adam was curious to see the hitherto unknown world under the tiles.

'I never imagined there wasn't some perfectly simple explanation,' Peter assured her.

'I should hope not!' But he was looking relieved, all the same, and she added hastily, 'I've told *you* because we're friends, as you reminded me just now, but I'd be obliged if you'd keep it to yourself. There's no need for you to feel you ought to pass it on next time anyone gossips about me. I really couldn't care less what they say, and I'm sure Mr Delaney couldn't either.'

'He can take care of himself, but I'm not so sure about you, Jan.'

What on earth did he mean by that? Aware that she had wasted enough time, she turned on her heel with an angry flounce and went off to get some breakfast. The conversation with Peter had annoyed her out of all proportion to its importance, but she was glad, nevertheless, that she had made that early visit to the ward, because she met Adam, arriving unusually early.

Very well turned out in a medium grey suit and green-and-white striped shirt, he halted at once and, without any conventional greeting, demanded to know whether she had news of Caroline.

'She had a good night, and I don't think there's any immediate cause for alarm——'

'Don't be ridiculous!' He was very much the top-notch consultant talking down to a mere house surgeon. 'With anyone in Caroline's state there's always cause for alarm. One must always be prepared for the worst.'

'You mean—she might die quite suddenly?'

'That's precisely what I do mean. I thought I'd explained to you how very grave the situation is?'

'Yes—yes, you did. I'm afraid I hadn't fully grasped it.' Jan paused, wondering whether she might risk another question which could easily turn out to be extremely stupid. Yesterday she wouldn't have hesitated, but Adam was a different person altogether this morning.

'If Caroline had a transplant,' she began slowly, 'would you do it yourself, here at Amberwell?'

She was gazing up at him intently, her green-flecked eyes wide and full of concern. On the verge of another explosion, Adam checked himself. For a moment he held her gaze as memories of last night washed over him and he longed to repeat the sweet experience which had been so rudely interrupted by the tractor driver.

But even someone as intolerant of gossip as he was could hardly fail to be aware of the inadvisability of kissing his house surgeon right there in the front hall of the hospital!

And so he tightened his lips and merely said curtly, 'Of course not. Caroline would have to go to Harefield. And now, if you haven't any more silly questions for me, you'd better get on with your morning round. I shall want an up-to-date report on every one of my patients later on.'

CHAPTER NINE

AFTER a few days in the side ward Caroline was moved, at her own request, to the main ward, where her fragile loveliness at once made her a general pet. Although the other patients did not know how close she was to death, they seemed to sense it, and there was always somebody talking to her, or arranging her flowers or making sure the television was tuned in to the programme she wanted to see.

'I'm getting thoroughly spoilt,' she said to Jan one day in her weak breathless voice. 'I shall miss all this attention when I've had my transplant and I'm learning to live an ordinary life again.'

'I expect you'll soon adjust to it,' Jan told her with a smile that struggled to hide how much she wanted to burst into tears. Doctors weren't supposed to cry in front of a patient. It would be unforgivable!

'If only it wasn't such a long, long wait!' Caroline sighed, and leaned wearily back against her pillows.

It was hard to think of a reply to that, and Jan had to make do with something vague about it happening when it was least expected. Of course it would be unexpected! A new heart would almost certainly only become available as the result of an accident to someone else.

Cross with herself, she went into Peter's office to recover her equilibrium and found him there busy with paperwork.

'You look upset,' he said, his grey-blue eyes studying her keenly. 'What's the matter?'

'Caroline.'

'I might have guessed. I'm always finding my nurses mopping their eyes in obscure corners. I've never known anything like it.'

'It's because she's so young and pretty and *nice*, I'm afraid. If she was twenty years older and plain and bad-tempered, nobody would feel so sad about it. It isn't fair.'

'Of course it isn't fair, but it's human nature.' Peter put down his pen. 'Changing the subject, Jan, my mother's coming home tomorrow. She's had nearly three weeks at the Anchorage and seems to have made a good recovery after her attack. The thing is, I'm worried in case she should overdo it getting the house back to the way she likes to keep it. Most of the time I shan't be there to stop her.'

'You'll have to read the riot act,' Jan told him.

'Easier said than done, but I shall do my best, of course.' He paused, looking at her thoughtfully almost as though he had something else to say but doubted the wisdom of it.

They had never regained the old friendly relationship after that Sunday evening when she had refused his lovemaking. Jan was sorry about it, for she was genuinely fond of him, but there was nothing she felt able to do to improve matters. Nor was she really sure she wanted to in case he got the wrong idea.

'I was wondering—' Peter started off again with unusual diffidence, 'could you possibly find time to pop in at lunchtime tomorrow and take a look round the house?'

'Round the house?' She stared at him in astonishment. 'Whatever for?'

'I want it looking OK when Mum comes home, but I'm not very good at that sort of thing. I've never had to bother, you see, until now. I've got some flowers and tried to arrange them, but—well, there are sure to be small details which only another woman would notice. So would you mind?'

Jan was completely taken aback. She had never been considered a domestic type, and she hurried to point that out. 'Surely you've been getting the house properly cleaned while your mother's been away?' she asked.

'Oh yes, I've been having a woman coming in regularly and I intend to keep her on. It's the little feminine touches that are worrying me. You could fix it to be away from the hospital for an hour, couldn't you?'

'I expect so.' Jan tried hard not to sound as reluctant as she felt. 'Luckily it's not one of Mr Delaney's operating days, but I shall have to tell Tim and make sure he'll be here.'

'I don't suppose he'll mind. He's an obliging sort of bloke.'

But unfortunately this turned out to be an occasion when Tim found it impossible to oblige his junior.

'Sorry, Jan—I've promised Vanessa to go with her in my lunch hour to look at some curtain material she's thinking of buying. I'm sure my opinion won't make much difference to her choice, but she's made rather a point of having it. Why don't you ask the boss to cover for you? He generally lunches here.'

Jan looked horrified. 'I wouldn't have the nerve!'

'Don't be daft. It'll be all right if he's not in one of his moods, and we haven't seen so much of those lately. Not since Julie left the hospital, now I come to think of it.' Tim's eyes twinkled at her. 'Might be a connection there, wouldn't you think?'

Jan nodded abstractedly, her mind on the coming ordeal. Though why it should be an ordeal she couldn't imagine.

Having located Adam in the car park, rubbing a duster over the windscreen of the Mercedes, she started diplomatically.

'Would it be all right if I went out tomorrow for an hour at lunchtime?'

'Barring an emergency at, say, twelve o'clock, I can't see anything against it.' He treated her to the charming, friendly smile which caused somersaults among the hearts of patients and nurses. It had exactly the same effect on Jan.

'Oh, thank you, sir.' She was about to continue, but Adam went on speaking.

'Got some specially important shopping to do?'

'Er—no, I'm not going shopping.' Her mind worked frantically and came up with nothing but the simple truth. 'Peter—that is, Charge Nurse Felgate—wants me to look round his house and make sure it'll pass muster with his mother. She's coming home tomorrow.' Adam's expression had changed and she began to babble. 'I told him I wasn't a bit domesticated, but he insisted and—well, I didn't seem able to get out of it.'

'No doubt you wanted to do what you could for him,' Adam said smoothly. 'I seem to remember you and he are rather special friends.' He half turned his back and resumed his polishing. 'I don't quite understand what the problem is. Tim will be here, won't he?'

'I'm afraid not.' Hastily she explained. 'That's why I had to come to you.'

'I see. Now we're getting the whole story. I can't think why you made such a mystery of it. It's quite natural to want to help your boyfriend with a domestic matter. As for needing cover for an hour or so while you're away from the hospital, you may rely on me.'

'Thank you sir,' Jan said again.

She turned away so precipitately that she scarcely heard Adam's muttered, 'My pleasure,' nor did she see the sarcastic twist which spoilt the clear-cut line of his mouth.

Nothing intervened to prevent Jan keeping her promise, and she left the next day punctually but with so little enthusiasm that she felt obliged to salve her conscience by buying an expensive pot plant on the way. Peter had had the whole day free, and when she entered the house she could see little with which to find fault. In her eyes it all looked painfully tidy, and the only thing she could think of to do was to remove the water splashes from the electric kettle. Even Peter's bunch of florists' flowers looked, to a non-flower arranger, very attractive in their big blue jar.

'Have you got to drive to the Anchorage to fetch your mother?' she asked, standing rather helplessly in the middle of the room.

He shook his head. 'She's coming in by ambulance, on its normal daily run between the convalescent home and the hospital bringing patients for treatment, etc. They reckon to be here about two-thirty.' He slipped a waterproof mat under Jan's cineraria and stood back to admire it.

It was nearly time for her to go and she was absurdly anxious to escape. Jingling her car keys in her pocket, she was just beginning, 'I think I'll be on my way——' when Peter interrupted.

'There's the ambulance now! You can't go for a few minutes, Jan.'

And so she found herself standing in the porch while Peter went down to the gate. As he got into the ambulance to collect the luggage, Margaret came slowly up the path.

'How lovely to see you, Jan!' She kissed her warmly and went with her into the house, clearly a little emotional at returning to her own home after so long.

Jan herself was feeling a surge of warm affection for this old friend who had once seemed almost like a mother. She said with genuine pleasure, 'It's wonderful to see you looking so well!'

'I feel wonderful, and so very happy to be back
and to see you and Peter waiting to welcome
me—almost as though you were married.' Margaret
hesitated and then went hurrying on as though she
were a little uncertain of the wisdom of what she
was going to say but intended to say it anyway. 'I'm
sure you must know it's always been one of my
dreams to see you and Peter together for good. To
my mind you're absolutely made for each other.'

Jan was appalled. As she tried to think of
something noncommittal and yet not unkind,
Margaret continued speaking.

'It's even more important to me now
because—let's face it—I could have another heart
attack one of these days and I might not be so lucky
another time. But if Peter had you with him——'
She left the sentence unfinished and gave the
distressed girl a tremulous smile.

'You mustn't worry about that sort of thing,' Jan
said gently. 'If you take your medication regularly
I'm sure you'll be all right. And now I really must
fly or I'll get into awful trouble for being late.'

She drove back to the hospital with very mixed
feelings, happy because Mrs Felgate was well again
and desperately sorry because she had this fixation
about her own marriage to Peter. Why did people
so often want to push other people around and
make them do things they didn't want to? There
was her father taking it for granted she was going
into general practice and quite unaware of her lack
of enthusiasm because he had never asked her what

she wanted. And now she was being urged into marriage with Peter, and she didn't want to do that either.

It was in a very disgruntled frame of mind that she parked her car and went into the hospital. Ought she to tell Adam she was back? As she debated the point, trying to persuade herself it wasn't necessary, she met him in the entrance hall.

He immediately bore down on her, but as Jan steeled herself to endure an interrogation concerning her visit to the Felgates' house, she discovered he had an entirely different matter on his mind.

'I've just been talking to your father, Jan—on the phone, of course—and we fixed up to sail together again next Saturday.'

He paused and Jan waited hopefully. She couldn't possibly join them, she knew that, but it would be nice to be asked.

But Adam went on breezily, 'I told him I'd discovered a registrar—the one on the thoracic team, Martin Blake—who's crazy about sailing, and the net result of the conversation was that Dr Latham suggested I bring him along. If he turns out to be useful, your father will have another ready-made crew for times when his usual mates can't make it.'

He had been talking with his eyes fixed on some spot beyond the top of Jan's head, but now he looked down and met her eyes as he waited for her to say something.

Jan forced herself to sound enthusiastic. 'That's

great! It's always worried me because Dad didn't get as much sailing as he would like. This arrangement you've made ought to just about double it.'

'I hope so.' Adam's gaze returned to the spot he had been studying before. 'No doubt you'll be glad not to get involved,' he suggested. 'I've rather got the impression you're lukewarm about messing about in boats.'

'I enjoyed it last time,' she said in a low voice.

But he had already turned away and her words did not reach him.

Jan sighed as she stood still for a moment staring after his tall figure. She had an unpleasant sensation of having been put firmly in her place, though nothing in their conversation actually indicated that. She knew she had been very much a temporary member of the crew on that golden afternoon which had ended so disturbingly. It was only natural that Adam should be pleased to have made other arrangements, and a registrar shouldn't find it so difficult to get away as a mere house surgeon. It was ridiculous to have this absurd sense of rejection.

The feeling persisted in spite of her efforts to crush it, and when Saturday came she was glad to be busy all day. Two cases of cardiac arrest in the town, a woman while shopping and a man who was playing in a cricket match, took up a great deal of her time since Tim was off duty and she was in charge. Very few of her thoughts could be spared for the three men on *Sea Lady*, and even the weather almost escaped her attention, though she did just manage to be glad it was a sunny day with a good wind.

Just like that wonderful Sunday afternoon.

She was not the only one to be reminded by the weather of the previous occasion. Robert Latham—not a man to be inclined towards remarks of a fanciful nature—had jokingly suggested that Adam must have some influence on meteorological matters, since they had again been blessed with perfect conditions.

'Beginner's luck,' Adam assured him.

'I would hardly describe you as a beginner.' Dr Latham's gaze moved to the new third member. 'Martin seems a useful man.'

'I reckon he knows more about it than I do.'

Robert made no further comment, but at the end of the day he lost no time in asking when it would be possible to fix up another sail.

The thoracic registrar grinned, showing white teeth in a tanned face. 'Tomorrow would suit me. The tide will be right.'

Robert could hardly believe his luck and he turned towards Adam. 'That be all right for you too?'

'I can easily make it so.'

The next day they were more adventurous and went right down the Amber to its mouth, returning tired and hungry only just before dark.

'I wish I could persuade you to come out for a meal,' Adam said, addressing his host. 'It would give me a chance to repay in a small way some of the pleasure you've given me.'

'I told you last time,' Dr Latham reminded him severely, 'I never go out for meals.'

'You could change your mind.'

'No, I couldn't, because I don't want to. It's not that I don't appreciate the offer,' he added hastily. 'I wouldn't enjoy it, that's all. Why don't you two young chaps go off on your own?'

'You can count me out,' said Martin. 'I've got a very patient and understanding wife at home. I don't want to push my luck too far.'

'That's it, then.' Adam plunged into his dark blue guernsey and emerged with his hair on end.

'If you really want to take somebody out for a meal,' came Robert's voice from behind, 'why don't you ask my daughter? She's got a healthy appetite and would really appreciate it.'

There was a short silence and then Adam said doubtfully, 'I'm not sure if she would want to come.'

'Try her and see. It's my bet she'll jump at it. You work her terribly hard at that hospital of yours and I reckon she's earned an outing.'

'Well, if you put it like that—perhaps it would be a good idea. It's too late to ask her this evening, but I'll try and fix it for another time.'

Thinking it over on the way home, Adam found himself liking the idea more and more. It would be a nice gesture towards Jan's father, who seemed keen on it, and it would show her that he appreciated her hard work.

Having convinced himself there were excellent reasons in favour of the invitation, Adam was able to ignore that other reason which, firmly repressed and yet daily growing stronger, had nothing to do with Dr Latham.

He was very much in command of the situation when he waylaid Jan on Monday morning. They had met in the long corridor which ran from front to back of the hospital and there was constant traffic of nurses and porters past them as they stood talking.

'I wanted a word, Jan. Can you spare me a minute now?'

'Yes, of course, sir.' She looked up at him expectantly.

The weekend's sailing had deepened his tan and his dark blue eyes were brilliant with health under the thick black lashes. The tiny sun creases were very much in evidence, and even his dark hair seemed to have been lightened by exposure to sunshine. He looked strong and virile, and Jan's wayward heart was sending the hot blood coursing through her body in response to his maleness.

'It would give me great pleasure—' he had never sounded so formal '—to take you out to dinner one evening this week if you could make it convenient.'

'Oh!' The shock seemed to have paralysed her tongue and for a moment she couldn't think what to say to him.

Adam's gaze raked her astonished face. 'Which day would be best?' he asked, taking it for granted she would accept.

He was right about that. In spite of her amazement, it never occurred to her to refuse.

'I shall have to make sure Tim can cover for me.'

'Naturally.' He paused, apparently thinking. 'Wednesday or Thursday would suit me best, so see Tim about it at the first opportunity and let me know.' For the first time he smiled. 'And wear your best dress. We're going to the Granville.'

The Granville! Jan had never been there, but she knew it was the smartest and most expensive place in the neighbourhood. 'I'll try not to let you down,' she said humbly, dropping her eyes hastily in case there might be a wicked gleam in their green depths.

Adam looked at her suspiciously, sensing there was a teasing note beneath the apparent humility, but all he said was, 'The food is excellent there and as your father says you've got a healthy appetite, I hope you'll enjoy it.'

'Dad said that?' Jan's lashes flew up. 'He knows about the invitation, then?'

'He could hardly help knowing.' Just in time Adam saw where the conversation was leading him. No girl would relish being told her father had suggested she should be invited out to dinner. Nonchalantly, he added, 'I tried to persuade him to come too, but he refused firmly, just like he did last time. You'll let me know as soon as you can which evening it's to be, won't you?'

'Yes, of course.' She glanced up and for a moment her eyes met his. 'I shall look forward to it,' she said simply.

Her sincerity was obvious, and Adam felt more than ever glad he had avoided that pitfall. But as

Jan went on her way she was aware that her doubts were not entirely squashed. It would be just like her father to initiate the invitation and then add that remark about her appetite. He would see no harm in it at all.

And neither should she. Obviously Adam wanted to repay Dr Latham for some very enjoyable sailing, and if it had to be done this way she should count herself lucky and stop worrying about it.

Tim, as usual, was obliging and incurious—though Vanessa scolded him afterwards for not asking who Jan's dinner partner was—and the evening was fixed for Thursday. She was glad of that because it gave her an extra day in which to find time for buying a new dress. By going without lunch she managed it somehow and so became the owner of a particularly nice Indian cotton in what the shop assistant called 'dahlia' colours. She would have liked something slinky and sophisticated, but she had enough dress sense to know that wasn't her style. She just hadn't got the figure for looking slinky.

Her tawny hair needed no special attention. She wore it loose, glowing above the pretty neckline of the dress, and completed her toilet with long jade earrings and a string of matching beads.

'Quite a transformation!' said Adam when they met by arrangement in the car park.

Jan laughed up at him. 'Did you think I'd wear jeans and a sweater? You told me to put on my best dress.' No need to let him know she'd bought it specially.

His eyes told her she was looking attractive. He folded her cream fleecy wrap round her and handed her into the Mercedes with as much care as though her comfort was his one aim in life. Jan couldn't help enjoying it, even though she knew it rested on nothing more substantial than good manners.

Granville Towers—known locally as the Granville—had once been a country estate in private ownership. It was situated only a few miles from Amberwell and the mansion was reached by a long drive through a wooded park. Standing on a slight rise and blazing with light, the hotel received them into its opulent interior with a warm friendliness, and soon they were being conducted to the big restaurant built out at the back. Here the lighting was more discreet and there were tall plants with spreading branches to give an illusion of privacy.

Adam had booked one of the best of the smaller tables. Seated side by side on a green velvet banquette, they had their backs to the wall and could survey the scene or give their attention entirely to each other. Just as they liked.

At first Jan was happy to look about her, to enjoy the luxury all around and let Adam take the lead in choosing the food, assuring him she liked 'everything.'

That seemed to amuse him, and he asked her if she had an equally catholic taste in wine.

'I don't know much about it,' she said frankly.

When Adam had finished his long study of the menu and wine list they began to talk, at first a little stiffly but gradually with greater relaxation. The scene which had so fascinated Jan at first almost ceased to exist and she was aware only of her companion. His left hand, beautifully shaped with perfectly manicured nails, was so close she could have touched it with only a very slight movement, and his shoulder in the elegant dark suit was only a few inches from her own. During a pause between courses she found herself with a ridiculous longing to lean against it.

By the time they reached the coffee stage they were both aware of an odd sort of tension. Conversation, which had been easy and natural, seemed to have dried up. It was time to go.

Adam signalled to the waiter and paid the bill. Jan sat quietly waiting with her hands folded tightly in her lap, and it seemed to her that she had never been so torn by conflicting emotions. There was regret that the beautiful magic evening was over and she must return to normal life with its endless round of work. And at the same time she knew as certainly as though it had been put into words that everything wasn't over, the end wouldn't be reached until she got back to the hospital.

'Ready?' Adam glanced down at her. 'Then let's be on our way.'

CHAPTER TEN

ADAM had started out that evening with the best of intentions. He would do exactly what Dr Latham had suggested. He would give Jan the sort of treat that didn't often come the way of hard-working junior doctors, an absolutely first class meal in beautiful surroundings. And that would be all. When it was over he would drive her back to the hospital, say a sedate 'Goodnight,' and return to his flat.

It would be simplicity itself. Absolutely no problem.

But before they were much more than halfway through their meal he had known it wasn't going to be simple at all.

He was still wrestling with himself when they got in the car. The memory of that other occasion when he had held Jan in his arms and tasted the sweetness of her lips was fresh in his mind. He had been furious when the tractor interrupted them, but he had meant it when he said afterwards that it had been a good thing, or else he might have got carried away.

There was no doubt about the dangerous attraction she held for him. And it wasn't only physical either: he liked her independence and courage, the way she stood up to him sometimes, and she interested him because he thought she had great potential as a surgeon.

All that made him want to kiss her very badly indeed.

The battle was lost within minutes of leaving the car park. With a swift turn of the steering wheel Adam sent the big car into one of the narrow side turnings and they were instantly shut into a small secret world of their own. Trees crowded close on both sides, their trunks blocking the beam of the powerful headlamps, and above their heads the star-spangled sky showed only through a tangle of leaves.

'I don't think there'll be a tractor along here,' Adam said as he switched off the lights.

Jan made no reply, her heart was thudding too violently for speech. When his arms reached out for her she melted into them as naturally as though she belonged there. When his mouth found hers and became painfully urgent and demanding she pressed herself against him and gloried in bruised lips and crushed breasts.

Their embrace became still more passionate. Vaguely Jan realised they were near the point of no return, but she didn't care. Nothing mattered just then except the pleasure she and Adam could give each other.

He was the one who drew back. With a sudden swift movement he abandoned her mouth, and with his arm around her shoulders, turned her so that they both faced forward, his cheek against hers. He was breathing hard and they were silent for a moment. Then Jan was astonished to hear a small sound very much like a chuckle.

'I was just wondering what Charge Nurse Felgate

would have thought,' he murmured wickedly.

'Peter's got no right to think anything,' Jan asserted indignantly.

'I rather thought he had. That is, I did until just now. I don't believe you would have allowed yourself to—er—get carried away like that if there'd been anything serious between you and Felgate.'

'I hope I wouldn't.' Jan did not sound entirely certain. 'He's just a very old friend, that's all. I'm fond of him, but that's as far as it goes.'

'I'm relieved to hear it.' Adam hesitated and Jan waited for what was to come. 'I'm relieved, because that means we can repeat the experience another time, if you would—er—like to.'

Would she like to? At that moment it was what she wanted most in the whole world; nevertheless Jan couldn't make up her mind how to answer. Loud and clear in her head a warning bell was ringing and she knew that if they did repeat 'the experience' it would be unlikely they would be able to keep control of the situation.

Did she want to embark on an affair with her boss?

Part of her wanted to so much she didn't care about the wisdom of it, but her basic common sense told her it would be madness and could lead to heartbreak.

'You're taking a long time to reply,' Adam complained. 'I rather got the impression you were enjoying the last half-hour as much as I was. Or am I wrong?'

'You're not wrong.' Jan suddenly tossed caution

out of the window. 'And of course I'd like to repeat it.' Aghast at herself, she tried to put the brake on. 'What I mean is, that's the way I feel now, but I don't know if I shall change my mind later on when I've calmed down.'

'That goes for me too, so we'll leave it, shall we? See how we feel when we're on an even keel again?'

It was what she wanted him to say, Jan told herself firmly, but she didn't have to like it. She sat silently in her corner as he backed carefully out of the narrow drive into the wider one and turned towards the main road. His abrupt change of mood had bewildered her and it was hard not to feel hurt by it. She had no means of knowing that Adam's mind had followed the same path as her own with equal speed, and he too was uncertain of the wisdom of an affair.

For one thing, she was more than half through her six months at Amberwell and at the end of it she would go off to a new job. And for another, the affair might become more serious than either of them originally wanted, which meant somebody would get hurt. Adam didn't think it was likely to be himself. After the disaster of his marriage he imagined he was probably immune, but he didn't want to hurt Jan.

Consequently, when she lifted her face for his goodnight kiss he gave her only a light brush of his lips across her mouth and a quick hug. Torn between relief and disappointment, she slipped into the hospital by the side door and went to find Tim.

'Had a good time?' In the doctors' sitting-room

he took off his white coat and hung it on a hook.

'Super!' Jan flashed him a brilliant smile. 'Anything happened while I've been gone?'

'Nothing much. That hole-in-the-heart case in the children's ward was restless and I altered the medication slightly.' At the door he looked back with his hand on the knob. 'I haven't done your late round because I knew you'd want to keep tabs on the patients yourself.'

It was nearly midnight when Jan climbed up to her attic room. Worn out with emotion, she slept deeply, but as soon as the alarm awoke her all the events of the previous evening came flooding back.

She both longed for and dreaded her first meeting with Adam. Would he be any different? No, of course he wouldn't. She might have changed totally inside—a change, she now realised, which had been coming on for some time—but for him last night would have been no more than an incident.

Fortunately for Jan they met at the nurses' station outside Peter's office, with several other people present. She received no more than a taut, 'Good morning, doctor,' flung at her in an abstracted sort of way as Adam continued to study an X-ray, frowning as he did so. 'Have you seen this?' he barked at her suddenly.

Reading the patient's name upside down, she said, 'Yes, sir.'

'What do you think of it?'

Taking her courage firmly in both hands, she said boldly, 'The pulmonary valve appears to be malformed. I imagine it's congenital.'

'You would imagine right, doctor. I'm putting the patient on my next operating list.'

Jan was permitted to assist at the operation a few days later. Both on a personal and professional level she was thrilled to be helping Adam, and she was glad to discover that the job in hand claimed all her concentration. She might have been daft enough to fall in love with her boss, but at least it wasn't coming between her and her work.

Observing her absorption, both real and forced, Adam congratulated himself on avoiding a liaison which all his instincts had told him would be unfair to her. Perhaps he needn't have been so careful about her welfare? Perhaps it would do no harm at all to go out together occasionally and take things as they came?

He turned it over in his mind for a while and then found an excuse for approaching her on a personal matter.

Looking into the canteen at coffee-time one morning, he discovered her seated at a small table with Louise. By the time he had obtained his own cup, Louise had drained hers and was just getting up from the table, whereas Jan had only just started drinking.

'Hi, Jan!' Adam joined her, taking his welcome for granted. 'I've got something I want to discuss with you,' he announced.

Her heart missed a beat. 'Sounds interesting!'

'It certainly is to me.' He leaned his arms on the table and faced her. 'I'm thinking of buying a boat.'

'You are? That's certainly exciting. Do you mean

like Dad's *Sea Lady*? If so, I'm sure he'd——'

'Oh no, I can't be bothered with getting a crew all the time. I want one that's much smaller and easier to handle.'

'A dinghy, then?'

'Good God, no! I had one of those when I was at school, and though I enjoyed the discomfort then I wouldn't now. Actually, I'm not getting a sailing boat at all.' He paused to taste his coffee and grimaced. 'I'm buying a power-boat.'

Jan's face was a picture of consternation. She had been brought up to believe that sail was all-important and power-boats were a menace. They raced about undermining river banks and creating a wash that upset other people. Her father would be horrified.

'It's rather a surprising decision,' she said carefully.

'Not really. I've thoroughly enjoyed my sails in *Sea Lady*, but just being out on the river is what mattered to me most. I can get that so much more easily in a power-boat.' Discreetly and very briefly his fingers touched hers across the table. 'Am I forgiven now you understand?'

'Yes, of course.' The light touch of his fingers had done strange things to her heart and she knew her colour had deepened 'There's nothing for *me* to forgive, but I'm afraid my father will be shocked.'

Adam brushed aside Dr Latham's feelings on the matter and finally came to the point he had been aiming to reach. 'Will you come out with me in the boat, Jan? I'm getting it at the weekend. I'm sure you'd enjoy it if you could forget your prejudices. It really is a most exhilarating experience.'

She had no fears about her enjoyment, even if they only chugged along like the boats at Shinglewick which took you for a trip round the bay. And she had a whole day free on Saturday too. If she went to see her father in the morning, she could devote the rest of the day to Adam. If that was what he wanted.

He left her in no doubts about that, and when she returned to work she felt sure the warmth and happiness she carried within must be showing in her face. Nobody seemed to notice anything different, luckily, and eventually she was able to push to the back of her mind the joyous thought that in only two days' time she and Adam would be on the river together. Just the two of them.

On Saturday morning she was awake early, though she mostly slept very late when she had a free day. A glance at the window showed her grey skies and there was a damp feeling in the air blowing in, but so long as it wasn't actually raining it didn't matter. Adam could hardly expect his amazing luck with the weather to last for ever.

They met at the boatyard, and at first he seemed so absorbed in his new boat that Jan felt he had scarcely noticed her arrival. Men were like that, she reminded herself, and did her utmost to respond to his enthusiasm by admiring everything she could think of. It wasn't difficult, for *Bluebird* was a beautiful little craft, painted in two shades of blue and gleaming with newness.

'You won't go too fast along here, will you?' she

asked anxiously as, sitting close with shoulders touching, they left the quay.

'Scared?' Adam laughed, and opened the throttle a little.

'Not me. I was thinking of the swans.'

'I shouldn't dream of frightening them, but I hope you won't mind if I open her up when we're clear of the town.'

It was certainly exciting, and Jan loved every minute of it. Waves battered at the windshield and sometimes came in at the side of it, and the wind sent her hair streaming out behind her. Adam began to sing, roaring out a nautical song in a rich baritone, and she joined in. Helpless with laughter at their vocal efforts, they turned round at last and motored gently back to where they had started from.

When the boat had been moored, the cover put in place and everything made safe, it started to rain. Since they were both so wet already it hardly seemed to matter, but Jan was suddenly seized by a giant shiver.

Adam eyed her anxiously. 'Cold?'

'Not really. It was just one of those shivers that make people say somebody's walked over their grave.'

'Don't give me that rubbish!' He gathered up a handful of her wet, salt-encrusted hair. 'You may not feel cold now, but you're certainly going to take a hot shower before we even think about food. Me too, for that matter.' He looked at his watch. 'I'd no idea it was so late! There'll be no time for a proper meal out, but pub food would be OK. I suggest we separate now and get changed and cleaned up, and then meet here again at, say, half nine. Right?'

He saw her start off in her little car and then got into the Mercedes. As he drove to his flat he thought happily about the performance of his boat—which had come fully up to his expectations—and how very much it had added to his pleasure to have Jan to share it with him. He would have liked to round off the evening with a really good meal somewhere, but time had slipped away. His lips curved into a tender smile as it occurred to him that Jan wouldn't mind so long as she got fed!

Her wonderful health and zest for life had been the cause of his originally being attracted to her. So different from Julie, who was always getting headaches and other minor troubles. He hadn't heard anything of her for quite a while, but with Julie no news was almost certainly good news. Anyway, he didn't want to think about her just now; he must concentrate on getting ready to meet Jan.

Nevertheless, as he turned on the shower the thought of his ex-wife was still lingering in his mind. Afterwards he wondered whether he had had a premonition.

Clean and fresh, newly shaved and dressed in expensive lightweight trousers and green silk shirt, he was brushing his hair before the mirror when the telephone rang.

Adam's first thought was that it might be Tim phoning to alert him because of some particularly difficult emergency—Caroline perhaps, though he hoped desperately it wasn't that. There was so very little they could do for her now.

The moment he lifted the receiver he knew it wasn't Tim. Even before he could say his name, a well-known high-pitched voice assailed him, sounding more strident than usual due, he suspected, to panic.

'Oh, Adam, I'm so glad I've caught you! I rang earlier, but there was no reply except from that horrid answering machine and I just hung up again——'

'What's the trouble?' he asked in a resigned tone. 'I hope it's nothing that won't keep, because I'm just going out again.'

'You can't do that! At least, you can, because I want you to come straight round here. Oh, Adam, I've got that dreadful pain again. I'm in such agony——'

'Calm down, for goodness' sake! You can't be in real agony or you wouldn't be able to make a phone call. You'd be rolling on the floor.'

'But I was doing that earlier, only I took some painkillers and they kind of dulled it. I've just taken some more.'

'How many did you take?' he asked sharply.

'I don't know. I meant to take two or three, but I was in such a state I got in a muddle.' Her voice changed. 'I do feel a bit funny, Adam. Please come round quickly.'

He had no alternative—he could see that quite plainly. He might not love Julie any more—had, in fact, never loved her truly—but he couldn't desert her now.

There was also Jan to be considered. Should he bank on spending only a few minutes with Julie and then rushing off to keep his date with Jan? Much as he longed to do that, he knew that this time his ex-wife might be really ill, in which case Jan would be kept waiting down at the quay wondering what on earth had happened to him.

Better to phone her at the hospital and stop her going out.

He leapt to the phone, hung on in rising fury and despair as the operator rang the attic room, and then replaced the receiver with a sinking heart as she reported, 'No reply.' He would have to meet Jan as arranged, break the news to her and then abandon her to spend what remained of the evening as she chose.

No cosy tête-à-tête meal in some cheerful pub and—much, much more disappointing—no enjoyable session in some dark and tractor-free spot.

Jan was huddled in her car under the hood, listening to the rain drumming above her head. When the Mercedes swept up beside her, she opened the door and started to get out, but to her surprise Adam squeezed in beside her. In a few curt sentences he told her what had occurred.

'You do understand, don't you?' he finished desperately.

Jan was silent. It seemed to her at that bitter moment that she understood only too well that he would never be free of Julie's clinging. Because he was basically kind, and also—as in this case—because he was a doctor, he would always respond to an appeal for help. It just wasn't in his nature to refuse.

'Jan! For God's sake, say something!' Adam urged.

She pulled herself together. Of course he had to go and investigate the trouble. There was no way he could have refused. 'Yes, of course I understand,' she assured him, trying hard not to sound as forlorn as she felt. 'I'm just sorry it's put paid to that pub meal you promised me. You can't imagine how hungry I am!'

Her attempt at a laugh nearly turned into a sob. When he snatched at her with the desperation born of a different kind of hunger, she buried her face in his shoulder and clung to him until her forced her head up and captured her lips.

The embrace lasted only a moment and then Adam tore himself free. Jan sat still in her car until the Mercedes had purred away, then drove herself sadly back to the hospital.

Adam let himself into the pretty little Georgian house and went straight upstairs. The scene in the bedroom reminded him vividly of that previous occasion as he looked down at Julie lying white-faced on the double bed, the duvet pulled up to her chin.

'You've been ages!' she moaned.

'I came as soon as I could.' He took her wrist in a firm grip and counted the pulse. It was a little fast, but nothing serious. 'Now let's have a look at your abdomen,' he ordered.

He palpated carefully, taking a long time over it. There was some distension but no great tenderness, and it scarcely seemed that she had been in such pain that she needed to take painkillers.

'Where's that bottle of tablets you mentioned?' he asked abruptly.

Julie raised her head and looked vaguely round. 'I—er—think I left it in the bathroom.'

'And you still can't remember how many you took?'

'Not really.'

Adam went into the en-suite bathroom and soon found the bottle of Panadol. It still seemed almost full, and as he stood thinking, holding it in his hand, a horrible suspicion took root in his mind. He went straight back into the bedroom.

'I believe you've been doing a bit of fantasising, Julie,' he told her curtly. 'I'll accept that you've dosed yourself with these, but I don't think you've taken more than you should. It's my opinion that you made that up just to make sure I'd come running.'

She gazed up at him with huge eyes and he read her guilt plainly in them. With a furious gesture he thrust the bottle into his pocket.

'I'll take these with me, so there'll be no mistake, and I shouldn't advise you to make up any more fairy stories, because I'm not in the mood to listen to them.'

'But what about my terrible pain?' she wailed.

'I don't think it is terrible, but you're in need of a check-up. See your doctor on Monday and he'll probably fix it for you to have an appointment with Manning.' Turning on his heel, Adam strode to the door, but as soon as he reached it his heart smote him. 'If the—discomfort gets worse, you'd better give me a ring in the morning.'

Afterwards he cursed himself for weakness. He was as sure as he could be that Julie was in no danger, so why was he giving her an opportunity to make a nuisance of herself again—offering it to her on a plate, in fact? If he didn't take a firm stand, she would go on plaguing him for ever.

Somehow he must find a way of escape from the clinging tentacles of the past.

CHAPTER ELEVEN

ADAM slept badly yet nevertheless woke up early. For a while he lay stretched out in bed, reluctant to start the day.

For one thing, Julie was almost certain to ring up, and he dreaded having to cope with her in her present state. If he hadn't taken up medicine it would be so much easier to opt out of her life completely, but the mere fact that he was a doctor gave her a claim on him which he couldn't ignore.

With an effort he put Julie out of his mind, only to find her place taken by Jan—another problem of an entirely different kind. His body ached for her with a desperation that alarmed him. If only their evening hadn't been wrecked—Julie again—he would have been lying here with completely different thoughts running through his head, or so he hoped. Much pleasanter ones.

With an angry gesture Adam flung the duvet back and got out of bed. Fortunately he had a date with his squash-playing friend later that morning and by lunchtime he expected to have worked off some of his annoyance and frustration.

He was towelling himself after a shower when the phone rang. Reluctantly, Adam lifted the receiver, barked, 'Delaney,' into it and steeled himself. It was, as he had expected, Julie, but her first words surprised him considerably.

'Goodness, Adam, how terribly cross you sound! What's the matter?'

Her light, rather childish voice was completely different from the complaining tone she had used last night, and his mood immediately altered to match.

'Nothing's the matter. How are you feeling?'

'The pain's nearly gone, so I don't think I shall bother to see the doctor tomorrow. It seems a bit silly when I'm so much better—don't you think so? Besides—' she went rattling on, 'I don't want to worry about tummy pains when I've had such a lovely invitation——' She paused to heighten the effect.

'Invitation?'

'Yes—from your patient, Captain Steadman. He wants to take me for a drive and then out to tea at the Grand Hotel at Shinglewick. We've kept in touch since we were both discharged from the hospital, but this is the first time he's asked me out. When the phone rang quite early this morning I thought it must be you. I know you must have been worried about me last evening.'

Adam was so delighted about her news that he found himself admitting he had been seriously concerned. No need to add that his concern had been on more than one count! He made an unsuccessful attempt to get Julie to agree to a checkup and then replaced his receiver.

As he dressed his thoughts flew to Captain Steadman. He was old enough to be Julie's father—

was it possible he was seriously attracted to her? She could be very appealing when she liked, and an older man might appreciate her helplessness more than a man nearer her own age. He himself, after the honeymoon state was past, had found it utterly exasperating—and doubly so since the divorce.

As he got in his car half an hour later to drive to the squash courts, he noticed for the first time how very incongruous his white shorts and sports shirt looked in the sober and elegant Mercedes. Jan's little open car would have matched both his clothes and his mood far better, but he knew he would see neither it nor her today since she had told him she was on call for twenty-four hours.

He was wrong about that.

At the hospital Jan had also started the day in a mood of depression—a rare state of affairs with her. Sunday stretched ahead of her, empty and boring, and she was ashamed to find herself wishing something interesting would happen so that she had plenty to do. Unfortunately, something interesting for her might mean tragedy for someone else.

Louise was also on duty and they breakfasted together, lingering over the meal and commiserating with each other over the hard life they had to lead.

'When we're registrars we shall get most weekends free.' Louise scraped the inside of her grapefruit to extract the last drop of juice. 'I reckon I might start applying after one more houseman job. How about you?'

'After my next houseman job I shall take another and then go into general practice,' Jan reminded her.

'So you will—I forgot. Have you begun writing applications yet? It's not a bit too soon.'

Jan had known she ought to be thinking about the future, but she was obliged to confess she had done nothing about it. She put up with Louise's scolding and made no attempt to explain why she had been dilatory. It would never do for Louise to guess that the thought of leaving her present boss was so painful she couldn't bear to dwell on it to the extent of looking for a post which would take her away from Amberwell.

She would obviously have to take herself firmly in hand and begin searching through the adverts, or she might find she had no job to go to when the present one terminated—a disaster which she dared not even contemplate.

She would make a start that very afternoon, she decided. Sunday was usually peaceful, with the hospital full of visitors and doctors keeping well out of sight unless sent for to deal with an emergency.

Accordingly, she settled herself in the sitting-room with a pile of papers and magazines of a professional nature. She was alone and it should have been easy to concentrate, but unfortunately the mere fact that no one else was there made it harder to keep her mind from wandering. Regrettably, it always seemed to wander in the same direction, and no matter how frequently she reminded herself there could be no future in such dreams her rebellious heart continued to control her thoughts.

At four o'clock she made herself a cup of tea, and

then, cup in one hand and pen in the other, made a determined start on her list. As she wrote down the first name she was vaguely aware of the shrill note of an ambulance siren floating in at the open window. It was a common sound and it scarcely registered except to cause her to hope briefly that it wasn't a cardiac emergency.

Time passed and Jan's list grew longer. She was just thinking it was long enough when the door burst open and Louise stood framed in the doorway, unconsciously striking a dramatic pose with her hand on the knob.

Jan looked up vaguely and instantly became aware of tension. She refocused her eyes, which felt bleary after so much staring at print, and looked curiously at her friend, discovering in Louise's face a strange mixture of excitement and horror.

'Is something the matter?' she asked quickly. 'You look sort of shattered.'

'I'm not surprised.' Louise came into the room and flung herself into a chair. 'Make me a strong black coffee, there's an angel. Instant will do—it's quicker. I'd rather have a brandy, but there's no chance of that.'

Jan plugged in the kettle and measured coffee into two cups. As she waited for it to boil she again studied Louise. 'Is that blood on your white jacket? You'd better get a clean one.'

'Well, it's certainly not red paint.' Louise lifted her arm and studied the lurid smear. 'I'll change when I've had my coffee—I shall feel stronger then.'

'I wish you'd tell me what's happened,' Jan

complained. 'Or are you deliberately working me up into such a state of curiosity that I shall probably explode?'

'OK—I give in.' Louise cast a disapproving look at the scattered papers on the floor. 'While you were lounging in here doing a bit of quiet reading, some of us had to slave, and it wasn't pleasant either. I've never worked in an A. and E. Department, and I never intend to if I can help it.'

'How did you get involved?' asked Jan.

'The RSO is off today and so's his registrar, and the Casualty Officer was a locum and pretty young and inexperienced. Anyway, when the ambulance arrived he sent for help, and I was the one who had to answer the SOS. You know what it's like at the weekend with so many pe ple off duty.'

'Were you able to cope?'

'I had to, didn't I? Anyway, one of the casualties was definitely d.o.a. and the other——' Louise broke off and put out her hand for the cup Jan offered.

'The other was still alive?'

'Barely.' Louise shuddered. 'The head injuries were horrific!'

Jan took a sip of her own coffee. 'Do you mind if we re-cap? I take it we're talking about a road accident and two people were involved? Or were there more?'

'Just the two—thank goodness. The ambulance men said there wasn't another vehicle mixed up in it, so I wondered, when I recognised the driver, whether he'd had a heart attack. He was one of your patients, Jan—that Captain Steadman who was in the private ward at the same time as Julie Delaney. I got to know him then.'

'Captain Steadman? Oh, I am sorry—he was a nice man. The boss will be sorry too——' Jan came to an abrupt stop, struck by a strange expression on Louise's face. 'What's the matter now?'

'You haven't asked me who the passenger was, the one with such severe head injuries.'

'I hadn't got round to it yet. You haven't even mentioned whether it was a man or a woman——'

'A woman, and it's my bet she hadn't been wearing her seat-belt. They said she was flung through the windscreen. She was quite unrecognisable, but one of the nurses found her name in her handbag.' Louise's voice changed and Jan got the impression that, in spite of her state of shock, she was going to enjoy creating a sensation.

'The woman in the passenger's seat, Jan, had also been in the private ward recently. It was Julie Delaney, your boss's ex.'

Jan felt the colour draining from her face. She put her cup down carefully and leaned back in her chair. Louise was looking at her expectantly and she knew she must say something.

'I didn't know they knew each other,' she managed at last, and was surprised at the calmness of her voice.

'They got acquainted when they were in hospital and obviously they kept in touch. It's sad to think that her—friendship with him led to her death, but that's life, I suppose.'

'That might have been better put,' Jan

commented, 'but I know what you mean.'

'How will Adam take it, do you think?'

Jan had temporarily mislaid her voice. She had hardly got around to asking herself that question and she couldn't think of anything to say to Louise which wouldn't be the merest platitude. So she simply shrugged and left the question unanswered, asking one of her own instead.

'Is there really no hope for Julie? I don't see how you can be sure.'

Louise shuddered. 'If you'd seen her——'

'I'm very glad I didn't'

'You mustn't think I'm just giving you my opinion. We sent for the RSO, who was playing golf, and he confirmed it. She isn't quite dead clinically, but she soon will be. It's a matter of hours.'

Jan got up to make some coffee. She put her next question with her back turned. 'I suppose you also sent for Adam?'

'We tried to, but no one knew where he was.'

'He could be on the river. He's just bought a boat.'

'Well, I expect they'll get hold of him eventually.' Louise accepted a second cup. 'Nobody really knew what the correct procedure was with an ex-husband. If Julie'd married again there wouldn't have been any problem, but there doesn't seem to be anyone else close except Adam, her parents being in New Zealand.'

They went on discussing it, though Jan had begun to long for a few moments of solitude in which to somehow come to terms with what had happened, thrust it to the back of her mind and get on with her early evening round.

Eventually, since Louise seemed more relaxed, she made an excuse and escaped to her room. Crossing to the window, she leaned on the sill and drew in a long breath of fresh air. A sparrow came and perched nearby, twittering cheekily, and a procession of white fluffy clouds sailed along above the chimneypots. In the distance a cluster of masts showed where the river lay hidden.

This time yesterday she had been there on the water, racing along in Adam's new boat, her shoulder pressed against his, her mood one of wild exhilaration. Yesterday she had been happy.

Her thoughts switched again to the man who had shared her joy in those carefree hours. Did he know about Julie yet? If so, how was he feeling? Deeply shocked, no doubt, as any ex-husband would be whether his emotions were involved or not, and she couldn't be sure that Adam's weren't. Certainly he had found Julie exasperating, but would he have so often gone to her rescue if his one-time love for her had been quite dead?

He was free now—completely free. But with a sigh Jan was forced to admit that it was more than likely he would choose to stay that way.

It was the first time she had admitted to herself the depth of her feeling for Adam. No longer was it a case of merely being sensually aroused by his good looks, his physical strength and the lean masculine virility of his body. She wanted all of him—mind

and spirit as well as body—and it was extremely
improbable she would ever possess any of it.

In spite of her unhappy thoughts, the brief
interlude of quiet had done her good, and she went
downstairs again feeling able to cope with a normal
Sunday evening. She did a leisurely tour of the
wards, finishing in Nightingale, where she spent a
few minutes talking to Caroline and making sure she
was not too exhausted after the inevitable afternoon
visitors.

The heart monitor showed disquietening signs,
but that was nothing unusual. The patient was
resting, her blue eyes, still lovely after weeks of
illness, fixed on the television screen. She greeted
Jan with a smile and waited in silence while the
chart was studied.

'Are you expecting any more visitors today?' Jan
asked with careful casualness, replacing it at the foot
of the bed.

Caroline shook her head languidly. 'Mum thought
I'd had enough this afternoon.'

'Very sensible of her,' Jan nodded approvingly,
talked for a little longer and then left.

Peter had been spending a rare Sunday on duty all
day and he came out of his office as she was passing.
At a casual glance he looked much as usual, but Jan,
who knew him so well, instantly detected a
suppressed excitement.

'Can you spare a moment?' he asked.

The request was normal enough, but the tone in
which it was said immediately captured her
attention. Whatever he wanted to say must be

important.

They had not met, except in the hospital, since the day his mother had returned home. Jan had taken it as a sign that he accepted—and maybe even approved—the fact that she wanted to end any possibility of romance between them. She now followed him into his office and waited while she closed the door behind them and made sure it was quite shut.

'I'll come straight to the point.' Peter began to walk up and down, shortening his strides to fit the small space available. 'It's all over the hospital that Delaney's ex-wife was involved in a serious car crash this afternoon.'

'That's right.'

Why *on earth* was Peter interested in that? Apart from being sorry, of course, as he would be about anybody's accident, it could have no possible effect on him.

But Peter was not thinking about himself.

'Further,' he went on, 'they're saying there's no hope at all for Mrs Delaney, though she's been moved to the ICU and put on a life support machine. It's only until her relatives can be contacted.'

'I hadn't heard she was in Intensive Care, but it's exactly what would happen. Louise told me about the accident——'

'Did she say the injuries were all on her head?'

Jan nodded. 'She described them as "horrific".' She studied him curiously. 'Why are you taking so much interest?'

'Can't you guess?' Peter allowed his excitement to bubble to the surface. 'I'm surprised you needed to ask me that question. To my mind, it sticks out a mile. It's what we've been waiting for!'

She stared at him blankly. And then, like an electric spark between them, an idea leapt from his mind to her own and she understood.

'Caroline!' she said softly. 'Oh, Peter, that's what you meant, isn't it? You're thinking Julie's accident might mean a chance of new life for Caroline?'

'Of course that's what I meant!' He stopped his restless pacing and seized her by the arm. 'There's no time to lose—they'll have to get permission from her next of kin, but Delaney ought to be able to see to that. Does he know about the accident yet, by the way? I heard they couldn't contact him.'

'They may have managed it by now.'

'In that case he'll be here at the hospital.' Peter let go of Jan and plunged for the door. 'Go and see if you can find him, and if he hasn't thought of a transplant for himself you'll have to sound him out. Go on—hurry!'

Jan was appalled at the mission thrust upon her. 'Why don't you ask him yourself? Caroline's one of your patients——'

'No way.' His tone denied her even the right to argue. 'I only know him professionally, but he's a friend of yours. Don't you go sailing with him in your father's boat? You're the obvious person to ask him. Get a move on, Jan—go and see if his car's in the car park.'

'I wish I knew what to say—how to lead up to

it——'

'Think of Caroline and what it would mean to her, and I'm sure you'll find the words will come.'

Wishing she could share his certainty, Jan passed him where he held the door open and went down to the side entrance. Normally the staff car park was full, but on a Sunday, with most of the important people taking the weekend off, it was easy to see at a glance whether the Mercedes was there or not.

It was not. Nevertheless, Jan still stood there, thinking deeply, and suddenly all her doubts and fears fell away from her and she desperately wanted to find Adam and talk to him about Caroline and Julie, and what one might be able to do for the other.

Disappointed because, now that she had found her courage, she desperately wanted to get on with it, she was just turning to go in when she heard the low purring of a powerful engine. The Mercedes swept up the drive and swung into the car park, drawing up just in front of her. Adam jumped out, still dressed in the jeans and sweater he wore on the river, and came striding towards her at the same moment as Jan plunged to meet him.

The bright evening light showed her his face and he looked like a man in shock. Before she could speak he hurled a question at her.

'What are you doing here, Jan? Did you want me?'

'Yes—and it's very important. Please, Adam, can you spare a minute?'

He frowned. 'I really am in a terrible hurry. I got a message to say my wife had had a serious accident.'

'My wife,' he'd said, just as though they were still married.

'I don't know the details,' Adam went on. 'I only got the phone message a few minutes ago, and all I was told was that poor old Steadman is dead and Julie very badly hurt. They were out for a drive together—she told me this morning they were going.'

'She has severe head injuries. They've put her on a life support machine.'

'As bad as that?'

'I'm afraid so.' Jan looked up into his face and saw that it had occurred to him for the first time that Julie might not recover. 'Adam, I know you won't want to talk about it just now when you're still suffering from shock, but it might be a good idea to think about—about Caroline, just in case——'

He stared at her blankly. 'Caroline? Is that why you wanted to see me? Has she taken a turn for the worse?'

'No, no, I didn't mean that at all. I was wondering whether Julie's accident might mean a chance for Caroline.'

It was said at last, and if Adam exploded into anger she couldn't really blame him. It certainly looked as though he might do that. His black brows had drawn together into a straight line and his mouth tightened.

He said tautly, 'Good God, Jan—you haven't exactly chosen the best moment to ask me that! I haven't had a chance to come to terms with any of it yet.'

'I know, and I'm sorry, but there really isn't any

time to lose. I felt terribly nervous about tackling you, but I kept thinking how wonderful it would be if—well, you know what I mean.'

'Yes, I understand. But I haven't yet got to the stage of looking at it objectively. I was married to Julie once, and that makes a difference.'

So he did still love her, and even if it was only a little he must be feeling terrible now. Tears stung the back of Jan's eyes and she winked them away determinedly, but she couldn't stop her voice shaking.

'I'm sorry,' she said again in such a low tone that Adam had to bend his head to hear her. 'I would never have mentioned Caroline at such a moment if it hadn't been urgent.'

He made no reply. He was staring at the ground with such a withdrawn expression on his face that Jan felt as though he had gone a million miles away. It made her feel desperately lonely and shut out, but she stayed there and waited in silence, knowing that he must answer her eventually.

At last Adam raised his head and looked straight at her. 'I'm glad you did mention it, Jan, and I'd like to thank you for it.' He began to move away. 'I must go now. I can't promise to keep you informed, but if there are any developments, no doubt the whole hospital will know about them within five minutes.'

CHAPTER TWELVE

'I'M AFRAID there's no hope at all,' James Manning said gently. He glanced across at Adam's set face. 'I'm sorry.'

The two men were taking up all the small space available in the cramped cubicle crowded with equipment. Between them on the narrow bed lay Julie's motionless figure, her head swathed in bandages and all around her an apparent confusion of tubes and wires connected to machinery.

It was hot in the Unit, but Adam felt himself shivering with nervous tension inside the thick guernsey he had worn on the river. He knew himself to be still suffering from shock, but nevertheless, his mind was beginning to clear and he didn't think he had ever experienced such mixed feelings about anything in his whole life.

Sadness still lay uppermost because of the terrible waste of life, and pity for Julie who hadn't known much real happiness during the last few years. She would never have a chance now to make something worth while out of the muddle.

But there was one thing she could still do.

Adam drew a long breath and felt his nerves steadying. He turned to the RSO. 'I want to talk to you, James. Can we go into your room?'

'By all means.' James Manning eased his portly

form out of the cubicle and led the way to his own sanctum on the floor above. 'Whisky?' he asked as he closed the door behind them.

'I could certainly do with it.' Adam watched as the drink was poured and then disposed of it in two gulps. He immediately felt better and more able to face up to the colossal task which lay ahead of him.

He began cautiously, 'First of all, I want you to give me your professional opinion on the state of Julie's heart.'

The RSO raised his eyebrows a fraction, but replied in a normal tone. 'There was some bruising of the rib cage, but the heart is quite undamaged.'

'That's what I was given to understand, but I wanted to make quite sure.' Adam leaned forward eagerly, placing his hands on the desk behind which James Manning was sitting. 'You'll have heard of my pet patient, Caroline Garnham?'

'Of course. In a small hospital like this such a case is known to everybody.'

'Then probably you won't be surprised at what I'm going to say now.' Adam paused and then continued slowly and impressively, 'Without a new heart she has no more chance of life than Julie with her terrible head injuries. I had her assessed at Harefield and the case is suitable for a transplant, but we've waited a long time for a donor.' Again he paused. 'There isn't much time left, James.'

Comprehension dawned in the eyes fixed on his face. 'You mean——'

'I mean there's every hope we've now found a donor.'

'Good God!' The RSO sounded almost awestricken. 'It's obvious really, but I must confess I hadn't thought of it. There's a great deal to do, Adam, and you'll have to act quickly. Er—have you the legal right to go ahead?'

'I may have, since she gave me as her next of kin when she was in hospital, but I wouldn't dream of proceeding without her parents' approval.'

'Aren't they on the other side of the world?'

'New Zealand, but I should have their phone number somewhere.' Adam frowned, thinking deeply. 'Perhaps I ought to ring Harefield first and have a word with the Transplant Co-ordinator.'

'I think you should. You won't, of course, say anything to the girl until it's arranged?'

'Definitely not.' Adam strode to the door. 'I know I can rely on you to keep this conversation to yourself, James.'

With James Manning's fervent assurance ringing in his ears, Adam ran downstairs and out to his car. It was clearly better to do the phoning from his flat rather than through the hospital switchboard, and he was bursting with impatience to make a start.

But first the Transplant Co-ordinator was off duty on a Sunday, though Harefield supplied a number at which she could be contacted, and then he had a long search for the New Zealand number. He found it at last and, dreading what lay before him, dialled it slowly and carefully. The conversation which followed was every bit as distressing as he had feared it would be, and he had to force himself to make his request. Strangely, that part of it was easier than breaking the news, and he sensed that Julie's parents might even derive some comfort from the knowledge that a vital part of their daughter could live on.

The next job was to phone the police and arrange for an escort. That done, Adam drove back to the hospital to make arrangements there.

He was surprised to find Peter still on duty, apparently even waiting in the hope that he might turn up. He put him in the picture as briefly as possible and then asked curiously, 'How is it that you already seem to know about this? I've got a strong feeling you're pleased but not surprised, yet no one knew about it except the RSO and myself.' Even as he spoke, light dawned. 'Jan told you, I suppose. I know you're close friends,' he finished.

'Yes.' Peter saw no point in admitting that the idea of a transplant had been his in the first place. The only thing that mattered was the agreement of all parties concerned and this had apparently been achieved.

They continued to talk in low voices, working out the practical details, and the two nurses on night duty left them severely alone, though both were intensely curious and sensed the tension.

Faintly, across the rooftops of the sleeping town, the church clock boomed out midnight. The hospital slept too, unaware of the drama building up in Nightingale, but up in the attics Jan had never felt more wide awake. She had taken off her white jacket and untied the ribbon confining her hair, but at that stage in her preparations for bed she came to a halt. It was *hours* since her conversation with Adam in the car park. Surely some decision must have been taken by now? She just had to know what it was.

Peter would be able to tell her. If they were going ahead with the transplant he must have been contacted by now. She had paid a brief visit to Nightingale earlier, to report on Adam's reaction, and had left him excited and hopeful, declaring his intention of remaining all night if necessary.

Putting on her jacket again but leaving her hair loose, Jan opened her bedroom door cautiously and ran downstairs. She slipped into Nightingale like a ghost and immediately saw the two men talking by the nurses' station. The mere fact of Adam's presence told her that something was happening.

Both men turned to look at her and she said eagerly, 'I just had to come and find out—I couldn't stop thinking about it——' Her voice died away and she had a swift impression that they had completely forgotten her existence and were taken aback to find her there.

'Come here!' Adam ordered curtly. 'I don't want to shout it out to the whole ward.'

He was suffering badly from reaction now that he had done all the most difficult part. As Jan approached nervously, looking like a child with her hair hanging round her face, his tone softened slightly but still remained businesslike.

'A transplant is to be attempted,' he told her tersely. 'We shall be leaving for Harefield in about two hours' time.'

'That's wonderful news!' Jan was so excited that her eyes sparkled like green fire and she almost forgot to keep her voice down. 'If you're going too, sir, I suppose you'll be able to watch the operation?'

'I certainly hope so.'

Envy seized hold of her and for a crazy moment she longed to accompany him. To witness a heart transplant actually being carried out would be such a wonderful experience. In the whole field of surgery she couldn't imagine anything more thrilling.

'How I wish I could come with you!' she exclaimed.

Adam looked astonished. 'It would certainly be out of the question. You're needed here to help Tim hold the fort while I'm away. I don't know at this stage how long I shall be gone.' He looked at his watch. 'I'll dash off home now and change into more suitable clothing. Can I take it, Charge Nurse, that you'll remain until we leave?'

'Definitely, sir.'

'As for you, doctor, if you don't want to do the sensible thing and get off to bed, you'd better stay here too. Caroline should be safe with both of you to look after her, in addition to the nurses.' On the verge of turning away Adam paused. 'But remember—not a word which might cause her to suspect anything should she wake. I'll tell her myself at the right time.'

'It really would be more sensible to go to bed, Jan,' Peter said when Adam had left them.

'That goes for you too,' she pointed out.

'Perhaps.' He hesitated and then added quietly, 'It so happens I've got a special reason for wanting to stay here tonight. Come into the office and I'll tell you about it.'

Puzzled, she followed him and sat down on a chair while Peter perched on the edge of his desk. As she gazed at him expectantly, it occurred to her that he seemed embarrassed.

'It's like this——' He thrust his hands into his pockets and stared down at the floor. 'During the last few weeks I've—er—er—become very fond of Caroline. She doesn't know, of course, and she mustn't either. Not yet, anyway.'

'You're in love with her?' Jan jumped up and kissed him impulsively. 'Oh, Peter, that's wonderful—at least, I'm sure it will be when——' She floundered to a full stop.

He smiled wryly. 'I'll let you know when congratulations are in order. Until then I hope you'll treat this as absolutely confidential——'

'Of course I will!'

'You don't mind?' he asked suddenly after they had been silent for a moment, both busy with their thoughts.

'Good heavens, no! You and I never had anything serious going for us.'

It was on the tip of her tongue to tell him about her feelings for Adam, but she restrained herself. There was no point in it. None at all.

A tap at the door heralded the arrival of the night junior with an offer of coffee, and both accepted gratefully. While it was being served Peter took the opportunity of telling the nurses what was going on. Their excited comments took up a little time, but after that there was nothing to do but drink more coffee and wait with as much patience as they could muster.

Adam came at last, looking very professional in a well-cut dark suit, and with an overnight bag in his hand. His manner was calm and almost detached. just as though he were setting off to some medical conference rather than a desperate dash across country with a life-or-death situation at the end of it.

Together he and Peter manoeuvred Caroline's bed out of the ward without disturbing anyone. She roused as they came into the lighted area, but Adam—whom she trusted implicitly—was immediately at her side. He held her hand in both his own and told her quietly what was to happen, and she listened with equal calm. After all, it was what she had been waiting for.

'You wouldn't think she *could* be so composed,' the junior whispered shakily.

'She's drugged to the eyeballs,' explained the staff nurse in a matter-of-fact voice belied by a sniff and a sudden groping for her handkerchief.

Jan, too, was on the verge of tears. The poignancy of the brief scene had been highlighted by the surface calm and they were all affected by it. She suspected that even Peter was struggling with strong emotion.

'Let's go down and see them off,' he suggested when he had controlled himself.

They ran down the stairs and arrived nearly as soon as the lift. Caroline's mother was waiting near the back door which the ambulance men used, and she also had her emotions tightly reined in. Within a few minutes the patient had been transferred to a stretcher and loaded into the ambulance.

As Peter and Jan went outside she noticed a faint lightening of the eastern sky which heralded the dawn. Was it a sign of new hope for Caroline's blighted life? Slightly ashamed of such a fanciful thought, she decided against sharing it with Peter and stood silently beside him, watching the procession preparing to move off. It was led by the flashing blue light of a police car, with Adam's Mercedes coming last.

'God, what wouldn't I give to go with them!' Peter exclaimed in such an anguished voice that Jan put out her hand and clasped his tightly.

Suddenly he flung his free arm round her and drew her close, burying his face in the softness of her hair. They stood like that for a moment, so that neither of them saw the little procession disappearing up the back road.

Nor did they see Adam glance back as his car made a wide sweep round to enter the road. But he saw them plainly, illuminated by the powerful overhead light, and it was his last glimpse of the hospital before the long drive claimed his complete attention.

'Now for the waiting game,' said Peter as they went indoors again.

Jan was suddenly so tired she could hardly face the climb up to her room. How long would they have to wait for news? she wondered as she hauled herself up the steep stairs, and she found herself repeating over and over, 'Please, please don't let it be too long.'

It seemed an eternity.

For nearly twenty-four hours there was no news at all. Then Adam phoned to say the operation would take place the following day. After that there was another wait before he rang in jubilant mood to announce that everything had gone well and he would be back about lunchtime next day.

Jan awaited his return in such a turmoil of mixed feelings she hardly knew how to cope. But when they actually met, at the beginning of a ward round, he was so exactly the same as he had been when she first knew him—kind to the patients, taut and businesslike with his house surgeon—that she experienced a bitter sense of anticlimax. The only time he showed any sign of feeling was after his daily telephone call to Harefield.

'They're delighted with Caroline's progress,' he reported. 'It's early days yet, of course, but there's no sign so far of rejection.'

'Great!' Tim's bearded face was radiant.

'How long will it be before we can be sure the transplant has been a complete success?' Jan asked.

Adam's dark sea-blue eyes flickered over her face, cool, calm and almost uninterested, and his whole manner changed. 'It's quite impossible to answer that question, doctor,' he told her curtly.

She felt rebuffed and struggled to hide hurt feelings. What had happened to the special relationship she and Adam had built together? Why had it apparently fallen apart? Some deep thinking in the privacy of her room eventually produced an answer.

Last weekend must have been a traumatic experience for him and he would take a while to get over it. If, as time went on, he still seemed totally uninterested in herself, she would have to face up to the fact that the affair—if you could call it that—had never had any chance of growing and developing as she would have like it to do; had never, in fact, got off the ground at all.

So Jan set her teeth and tried to concentrate totally on her work. She applied for and obtained her next post—house physician at a big London hospital—and began to count the weeks which remained to her at Amberwell. Sometimes she longed for them to pass as quickly as possible, and at other times she would have liked to slow the clock down and prolong her last weeks as Adam's house surgeon.

The only bright spot during this unhappy period was Caroline's reappearance at the hospital, not as a patient but a visitor. She was pink-cheeked and her lips no longer had that blue tinge which had made her look so ill. The whole hospital rejoiced at her changed appearance, but to the cardiac staff it seemed a miracle.

Jan told her father about it on one of her brief evening visits. Dr Latham was interested, but not as impressed as she had expected.

'Pity it couldn't have been done at Amberwell,' he commented. 'I bet Delaney thinks so too.'

'Yes, I expect he does.' Jan hesitated and then asked a question which she tried to make casual.

'Does he still sail with you?'

'Now and then. Not so much since he bought that damn noisy power-boat, of course. Why ever he wanted to spend his money on a thing like that beats me!' Robert looked at his daughter rather more closely than usual. 'Are you extra tired, Janice? You've lost your sparkle.'

'I expect the hot weather is getting me down.' She forced a smile.

'When's your next day off?'

'Sunday week.'

'You'd better come on the river in *Sea Lady* if I can get a crew. The fresh air will buck you up no end.'

Knowing it would be useless to protest, Jan did not attempt it. She spent the next few days wondering whether Adam had been approached, hoping that he had and then dreading having to spend a whole afternoon in his company with things as they were at present.

And then, after all, it was nothing but a waste of time, because the weather changed totally shortly before her free Sunday. The sun disappeared and the wind dropped until it ceased to exist at all, with the result that what should have been early morning mist hung about all day. Except for the temperature it was more like November than August.

Sailing was definitely off, and Jan didn't know whether to be relieved or disappointed.

She had a long luxurious lie-in and got up in time to arrive at the bungalow for lunch. She was a little surprised to find her father had apparently gone out, since his car was missing, but she knew he liked to assert his independence by being at times somewhat unpredictable and was not at all worried.

She let herself into the house and settled down with the Sunday paper. Then she laid the table and explored to find what was for lunch. It was nearly two o'clock by now and she decided to have her own meal. By the time she had finished she had begun to feel anxious.

He was almost certainly doing a job on the boat and had forgotten the time, but she definitely needed to *know*, and the only way to find out was to drive down to the river.

In the town the mist had cleared a little, but down by the water it was more like fog. Nevertheless Jan could plainly see her father's car parked in its usual place while *Sea Lady* lay motionless at her mooring, apparently deserted.

'Looking for your dad, are you?' said a voice behind her, and she spun round to find the owner of the nearest boatyard addressing her. 'Went out in the dinghy, didn't he?'

'Did you see him, then?' Jan looked round wildly, her heart hammering, and noted that the little boat was missing.

'Course I did—soon after breakfast, it were. I told him I didn't think it was a good idea with the tide on the ebb, but you know your dad—got a mind of his own, he has. Said he was fed up with the weather and a good hard row'd do him good. "Not if it lands you on the mud," I says, but he just grunted and off he went down the river.' Behind him a phone began ringing. 'Excuse me, miss—I'll have to go and answer that. I'm on my own today.'

Jan stood there thinking hard. On such a dreary day, with no wind at all, there was very little activity on the waterfront. Mist hung over the river and visibility was no more than fifty yards. Down-river it might be even less and it would be very easy to lose one's sense of direction, particularly at low water with very little tide.

A patch of blue caught her eye. Adam's *Bluebird* was tied up at the end of a jetty and still afloat, since there was deep water near the shore just there. It was just what was needed for a rescue operation on such a day. But had she got the nerve to ring up the owner and beg him to help her look for her father?

Perhaps he had other plans for the afternoon. Perhaps he wasn't at home.

There was a public phone-box quite near. Stifling her doubts and fears, Jan hurried towards it. Her pulses were racing as she dialled the number, but as soon as she heard Adam's voice she managed to steady herself and somehow pour out a coherent account of what had happened.

'I'll be right with you,' Adam said crisply.

CHAPTER THIRTEEN

WHILE she was waiting, Jan fetched a nylon tow-rope from her car. The MG had once humiliated her by requiring towing, and she had bought the rope as a result.

'Good idea,' Adam said when he joined her, but apart from that one brief comment he wasted no time on words. Within a few minutes they were motoring gently down river and Jan tried to give her full attention to searching the oily grey-green mud for a patch of scarlet which, she hoped desperately, would be her father's favourite anorak.

But in spite of her anxiety the memory of that other trip in *Bluebird* kept thrusting its way into her mind. Last time they had been singing, and laughing at their vocal efforts. Last time they had been happy. Or, more likely, it was only she who had been truly happy while Adam had merely been enjoying showing off his new toy.

Unconsciously she sighed, and Adam caught the forlorn sound. He glanced sideways at her and said encouragingly, 'Cheer up, Jan—we're sure to come across him soon.'

She did her best to share his optimism and a few minutes later it was justified. A breeze suddenly sprang up and the mist began to swirl instead of lying heavy like a damp grey blanket. At the same time there were little slapping noises from the water and a tiny wave reared up and splashed against the windshield.

'The tide's turned!' Adam exclaimed. 'The rate it comes in over these mud flats ought to make it a lot easier to float the dinghy when we find it.'

Jan wasn't listening. She thought she had glimpsed a patch of bright colour. And then, suddenly, she was *sure* something red glowed in the prevailing greyness and she turned excitedly to Adam.

'There he is! Look—over there towards the left bank.' She waved frantically and saw a hand lift in response. 'Oh, Adam, however are we going to get near enough to throw him a rope?'

'Can't tell until we find out which is water and which mud.' He turned the boat and proceeded cautiously towards that brilliant splash of colour.

They could see Dr Latham plainly now, sitting hunched in his tiny boat and watching their approach. Adam had found a narrow channel of clear water leading in the right direction, and soon they were close enough to try throwing the rope. This was clearly Jan's duty since Adam had to hold the power-boat as steady as possible.

After three attempts he lost patience with her.

'We'll have to change places so you can take charge of the boat while I throw.' He gave her rapid directions. 'Ready? OK then—I'll slide along the seat while you climb over me. Be quick about it!'

Jan was only too anxious to be quick, and because of that she was clumsy. She was so determined to get over his outstretched legs without collapsing on to his lap that she did exactly that. With the whole of her mind and body she was conscious of his body beneath hers—the strong firm masculinity of him. His face was so close to her own that she could see the golden tips of his dark lashes. She couldn't see his eyes because he had veiled them and there was a white line round his mouth where his lips had tightened. With a swift movement he gave her a push that sent her sprawling on to the other seat.

'Get busy, Jan,' he snapped, 'or we'll be aground too!'

Somehow, in spite of hammering pulses and an odd breathlessness, she managed to follow her instructions. Suddenly there was a triumphant shout of, 'Got it!' from her father, and then the curt order, 'Don't pull until I've made it fast.'

'Change places again,' Adam commanded, and this time she managed it more efficiently. Very gently he opened the throttle and Dr Latham's dinghy began to slide over the mud.

'Thanks very much.' It was plain the words were choking him. 'Never thought I'd have to be grateful to one of those damn things.'

'Would you care for a tow back?' Adam asked politely.

There was a pause and then Robert accepted the offer. 'But not all the way,' he stipulated. 'I'll do the last part under my own steam.'

'He must be feeling tired,' commented Jan, and this was confirmed when they were all back at the quay.

'You can do what you like with what remains of your day off, Janice,' her father said curtly, 'so long as you leave me in peace.'

Understanding that he needed time to come to terms with his humiliating experience, she merely nodded and said she would see him again soon.

'You seem to have been given the order of the boot,' Adam said carelessly. 'Er—would you care to come for a drink and a snack?'

Her mind was sensibly ordering her to refuse, but she was all heart just then and she accepted at once. But as they strolled towards his car she knew a moment of panic. What on earth would they find to talk about? Already the silence was becoming uncomfortable.

'It's splendid that Caroline's so well,' was the best she could manage.

'Yes, indeed.' Adam unlocked the passenger door and held it open for her. His face was like a mask as he stared across the top of her head.

Jan never knew what made her say the next thing. She was intent only on keeping the conversation going.

'Peter's so happy about it,' she told him brightly.

'Peter?' Adam got in beside her and fastened his seat-belt. 'Oh, you mean Charge Nurse Felgate. Well, I suppose he would be—Caroline was one of his patients.'

'I didn't mean that.' Jan hesitated, but felt compelled to continue. 'That night you took Caroline off to Harefield he told me he'd fallen in love with her.' She coloured slightly. 'I shouldn't really have told you—it's a secret at present.'

There was no reply for a moment. Jan had just time enough to decide she had been boring him when he answered her in a strange abrupt sort of way.

'I find this all very puzzling. It so happens that I looked back that night and distinctly saw you and Felgate locked in a passionate embrace.'

She stole a startled glance at his face but saw only a rigid profile. Adam appeared to be giving all his attention to his driving.

'Just to put the record straight,' she said crisply, 'it wasn't a passionate embrace at all. More for old times' sake, I suppose. Peter was feeling emotional and I was sorry for him.'

Again there was a pause, and then Adam said in a strangled voice, 'I see.' He was not at all certain what it was that he saw, but one thing was for sure—he'd got to find out. 'Are you hungry?' he asked suddenly.

'H-hungry?'

'You usually are.'

'What a reputation I've got!' Jan's laugh was horribly artificial. 'Actually I don't feel in the least hungry just now.'

'Good.'

They had left Amberwell behind and were in the country. Adam swung the car off the main road and down a narrow one leading back towards the river. 'We need to talk,' he said tersely. 'We can go to the pub later.' Or perhaps not, he added silently to himself.

They came to a large sloping field used for car parking and family picnics. It was deserted after such a miserable day and he stopped at the bottom where a gap in the hedge gave a view of the river. After hiding for days the sun had appeared and the water glistened in the evening light. The feathery tops of rushes whispered gently in the breeze, and around their roots moorhens searched for food and called to each other.

But neither of them noticed the view or the pleasant riverside sounds. As far as they were concerned they were alone on a desert island.

'Oh, Jan—Jan darling—I've been getting it all wrong. I thought——' Adam broke off and swivelled round in his seat to face her. 'It doesn't matter what I thought, since apparently it was a load of rubbish. There's only one thing which needs to be said right now.' He drew a deep unsteady breath. 'I love you, Jan, so very much, and however you feel about me I've just got to tell you.'

'You—love—me?' she asked in a wondering tone, and it seemed to her that the whole world rocked about her because of what he had said. 'Is it really true?'

'Of course it's true, darling idiot!' He moved nearer, his eyes raking her face. 'Would I say a thing like that if it wasn't?'

'No, of course you wouldn't. I'm sorry—it's just that——' She was suddenly illuminated by the most beautiful smile he had ever seen. 'It's only that at first I didn't feel I dare believe it. You see, I love you too, Adam, and it's so wonderful that you're the same way about me.'

Intoxicated by happiness, Adam reached out for her with a desperation that matched her own urgent need. She melted into his arms and reached up to draw his head down to the level of her own. Their lips met and clung while their hearts thudded in unison, and nothing had any reality for them except the sweetness and passion of their love.

Some time later they drew a little apart, their pulses still racing and the wonder of their shared love continuing to gild the whole world.

'I've loved you for a long time,' Adam said tenderly, 'but at first I struggled against it. After Julie, I didn't want to get involved again too soon. My first experience of marriage hadn't exactly recommended it to me.'

Jan's heart missed a beat. 'Does that mean you want us to—to have an affair?'

'No, it doesn't.' He broke off to kiss her again, more gently than before. 'I want you to marry me, Jan, just as soon as it can be arranged, and then after a little while—' his voice quickened with enthusiasm '—when Tim moves on, or I do, you can become my registrar. Just think—we'd probably be the only husband-and-wife cardiac team in the country!'

It was as though an icy hand had touched her on the shoulder and, unconsciously, she withdrew slightly.

'But, Adam, you've forgotten something.' Her voice shook but the resolution behind it was rock hard. 'I can't ever be your registrar, because I'm going into general practice. Here, in Amberwell.'

There was a long terrifying silence, and during it Jan slowly became aware that the real world beyond the cushioned comfort of the Mercedes had intruded into their happiness. The river was grey again now and the dying sun had vanished behind a bank of black clouds. The wind whispering in the rushes sounded eerie and cold, and Jan could not repress a shiver.

'I must admit I'd forgotten for the moment you were dedicated to joining your father's practice,' Adam said slowly. 'Are you really still sticking to it?'

'I have to. Dad would never forgive me if I broke my promise—and I wouldn't be able to forgive myself either. It means so much to him.'

Again he was silent. He stared straight ahead, frowning, and Jan's terror grew so that she started shaking from head to foot.

'Oh, Adam,' she begged, 'do please, please try to understand!'

He turned his head and stared at her face, white in the dusk, and suddenly her intense distress communicated itself to him. With a sudden gesture he flung his arms round her and drew her close, back into the warmth of his love.

'If I can only have you with strings attached, love, then I'll put up with the strings,' he said quietly.

When Jan had finished showing him how grateful she was in the way he found most acceptable, she said thoughtfully, 'Perhaps it wouldn't have been such a good idea for us to work together as well as living together. We'll probably have a better chance of happiness if we follow our own careers.' A sudden fear struck her. 'Didn't you say just now you might want to leave Amberwell one day? Whatever would we do then?'

Adam smiled with superb confidence. 'There's no way I could want to leave under present circumstances. I like Amberwell, its hospital and its river. And I shall like it even more when I'm married to young Dr Latham, GP.'